Christopher Carlisle is an Episcopal priest who takes 'heretic' literally: from the original Greek, 'hairetikos' meaning someone who is 'able to choose.' As one who never liked going to church, and who loves the secular world, his writing explores the romantic affair between God and humankind. Perpetually at odds with the hierarchy, he was turned out onto the street, where he created two outdoor communities in the renegade spirit of Jesus.

Amid street lights and burbling Harley-Davidsons, Carlisle launched Cathedral in the Night, an outdoor gathering of the homed and homeless around community, prayers, and a meal. So inspired his first novel, *For Theirs Is the Kingdom,* suggesting a radical reimagination of the institutional church. Carlisle earned his undergraduate degree from Columbia University, and graduate theological degrees from Harvard and Yale. A regular commentator on New England Public Radio, he is married with four children and lives in western Massachusetts.

For my beloved mademoiselle.

Christopher Carlisle

PICKETT'S DREAM

AUSTIN MACAULEY PUBLISHERS™
LONDON • CAMBRIDGE • NEW YORK • SHARJAH

Ordering Information
Quantity sales: Special discounts are available on quantity purchases by corporations, associations, and others. For details, contact the publisher at the address below.

Publisher's Cataloging-in-Publication data
Carlisle, Christopher
Pickett's Dream

ISBN 9798889103455 (Paperback)
ISBN 9798889103462 (Hardback)
ISBN 9798889103479 (ePub e-book)

Library of Congress Control Number: 2023918009

www.austinmacauley.com/us

First Published 2024
Austin Macauley Publishers LLC
40 Wall Street, 33rd Floor, Suite 3302
New York, NY 10005
USA

mail-usa@austinmacauley.com
+1 (646) 5125767

Like life itself, the novel demands too many people to thank. I'll try, anyway.

The invaluable nuts and bolts:
To my gifted editor, Lily Miller, whose belief in the story, against the odds, made me believe in it too;
To scholar and critic, David Staines, without whose boundless generosity I might have given up;
To Aaron Stryzewski, whose artistic genius knew the tale I only knew in words;
And to poet and teacher, Richard Wilbur, whose inspiration convinced me that "the past was never past redeeming";

My faithful band of heretics:
To Jim Clark, incorrigible madman priest who got me into this business;
To Armand Proulx, whose mystical vision sears the curtain between life and death;
To Mich Zeman, who helped me break the rules that needed to be broken;
To Lance Humphrey, Karen Skalla, Steph Smith and Eric Fistler, whose faithful work allowed us to build a cathedral;
And to Chad Wright, who was always at my side to make the outlandish schemes happen.

Without memorable characters in one's life, there would be no story to tell. So, I give thanks to three, however fictitiously rendered:

To Dave Nerkle, my inspiration for Pickett, whose memory lives beyond his death;

To Anneke Vandenbosch, my sixth-grade obsession with whom I didn't stand a romantic chance;

To a mean-spirited thirteen-year-old who gave me Ted "Tizzy" Talbot, and the hope that the prison sentence he just served makes for some kind of redemption.

Without the presence of friends to carry one through the ardor of writing a novel, it may not only have been impossible, but probably wouldn't have been worth it:

To Sid Poritz, who defines the difference between an acquaintance and a friend;

To Harris and Patricia Pastides, for their abiding friendship, especially when the chips were down;

To Tom Davis, who, when the chips were down, was my only running partner who would run six miles, then stop to have a cigarette;

To Dick Teresi and Cam Mann, whose "retrobate" claims couldn't be further from the truth;

To Steve Harris, whose quiet eloquence and humor made me feel like a Canadian brother;

To Baird Soules, whose quixotic vision of life reimagines what is possible.

Cary Grant once said, "Insanity runs in my family. It practically gallops." So, to my mother, Betsy, gifted writer and critic, for reading endless drafts and offering counsel at the ripe young age of ninety-five;

To my siblings, whose only insanity is their belief that they are "normal";

To my children, my greatest reassurance that tomorrow is sure to be better;

To my eleven grandchildren, who give me hope that life is worth the bet;

And of course, to Nathalie, my Mademoiselle, whom I am destined never to deserve.

I dreamt the past was never past redeeming...

—Richard Wilbur

In memory of Nerk

Chapter 1

On the day I graduated from college, my aunt said to me, "Brooke, you've been deprived—deprived of the need to work." It was one of those remarks that made me angry for countless reasons, but most of all because it was true. The fact is that none of the Adams of the Rhode Island clan has had to work since the Revolutionary War, when young George Adams first ventured beyond Europe to exotic Eastern parts unknown and returned on the high seas with a ship full of silk.

I wouldn't have taken the quip from any old aunt, however true it happened to be. But this was the aunt who had raised me from toddlerhood. If it hadn't been for her, I probably would have died on my third birthday.

The news came to my door as the party was ending. I remember because I was the only kid still wearing his party hat, and as my aunt would recount, the only human being she'd ever seen wearing one to bed. It was a last detail, she later explained, I just didn't need to worry about.

My father was a surgeon by profession and a committed churchman by vocation. Twice a year with my mother, he led medical missions to China, where he would spend a month in the rice paddies performing urgent surgeries on peasant farmers and their families. Their plane crashed on return, and as quickly as I came to know my parents, I was given to say goodbye.

Within the week, my aunt and uncle moved in, and together they embarked on raising the chubby child they never had. It was a fine place for a boy to grow up. Although the house sat squarely in the middle of Providence, the grounds that it shared with the Bishop's House lent the expanse of an enviable park.

If circumstance deprived me of the need to work, it never deprived me of the need to worry about the circumstances of others. The time God granted my privileged life to be concerned about the human condition has never seemed less than monumental. So, from the time I was eight years old, I have taken this to be my work.

It was then that I began to chronicle the eccentricities of my world. And to this day, this one stands on a shelf in Paris next to the twenty that preceded it. I must have been a disconcerting child to those around me, because only the likes of such a boy could ever have taken so detailed an account of the joys and failures of men.

At the end of college, I decided not to return to Providence. Giving in to the pressures of the Historical Society, I bequeathed it the great old house I had loved so deeply as a child. Perhaps it was a bid to cut myself off from those painful early years, or perhaps the need to ensure for eternity that no one would know the secrets I once knew, or breathe in the spirit of the place.

Several classmates on my floor had put together a scheme to start an American newspaper in Paris, and having written for the college daily, I was invited in. Paris was a city I had always longed to live in, so without a second thought, I set off for a life on the Left Bank. The enterprise was shaky from the beginning, but until it folded seven years later, I lived in the romance of knowing there was nowhere else I wanted to be.

As we packed up to go, I announced to my partners that I would be moving to Newport. They tried to persuade me to go with them to New York, and that having failed, advised me anything less than Boston would mean certain death. Why would I put down roots in a bygone summer resort, they wanted to know, even if it was the grandest town America had ever produced?

But this was the infamous 1980s, when the future lay no longer in recalling the past, but in proving beyond the shadow of a doubt that we were more than we were born to be. Every boy from Buffalo to Boise came East in the urban, resurrected hope that with his suit, his briefcase, and his small dose of brains, he would outstrip the next young pimply boy from Kansas City, Kansas. As one who was born to be skeptical of the enduring rewards of success, I was equally suspicious of this Eastern migration, and the promise that lay at its end.

And in fact, it was only a month before the stock market plunged to 'Black Monday' that I was treated to a fleeting glimpse of financial mortality. Sobered by the unthinkable truth that anyone can fall—that the way things are is not necessarily the way they will always be—for the first time in my untethered life I felt unutterably alone, as the childless end of the once prolific Adams family clan. In retrospect, returning to Newport may have been a last attempt to take account of whence I had come, and where it all might end.

Having given it most of the summers of my life, Newport lingered in my mind as my one true home, if not proof of who I was. The house had been the family homestead from before the Revolution, and I'd always perceived it as the single genuine place of our prosperous past. Except for improvements in plumbing and electricity seventy-five years ago, it had remained painstakingly untouched since the day of its completion.

The house stood on the edge of the historic district, which abutted the only commercial block outside downtown. There was a gas station, a post office, and in winter through the privet hedge, I had a clear view of the Rexall Drug Store. By Newport standards, the house would have been considered barely quaint, but its precarious leans, and many useless niches and turns, agreed with my present state of mind.

It was here that I penned the last diary I ever attempted. I had been in Newport just over a year, because the sweet melancholic lilac air was already gone from the front door, and the magnificent magnolia that filled my lawn was laden with voluptuous blooms. And indeed, the wedding where it all began was the second Saturday in May.

As well as I knew I could never love Athena in the way I had in the past, as I watched her car approach, my heart began to race like a love-sick adolescent's. If I had already accepted that 'what could have been' would never come my way again, I couldn't help but wish for a second chance at love with so beautiful a woman as this.

Yet, free from the complications of romance that can ruin a perfect day, I felt equally free to let down my guard and bask in Athena's beauty. In Newport, an Aston Martin was the kind of car a woman wanted to be seen riding in, but wouldn't be caught dead driving. Athena had little concern for such twists and taboos, or as my aunt would say, "the double-reversals of being rich. It is why," my guardian was quick to explain, with her tongue pressed deep into her cheek, "if you are truly wealthy, and the money is good, too big a house is out of the question."

"You're an escort to make any woman proud!" Athena called through the open window. Her bobbed mahogany hair was windblown from the ride and shone in the morning light. She reached across the passenger seat with the unabashed abandon of a ten-year-old girl, and I thought how her vitality never failed to intimidate me.

"Brooke, I love you for coming!" she said.

"And I love you for asking!" I said.

Athena's was a face that seemed always to be smiling— a spontaneous, incredulous, laughing smile she had managed to keep into her thirties. It was an enigmatic, elusive smile you could never be sure about, but which you utterly believed in as a last romantic outpost in an otherwise troubled world.

"That remains to be seen!" she ironically laughed, gently tossing her head. She had a lovely long neck. Her dark hair continued to hold the morning light, and her hazel eyes sparkled with delight.

Her skin was at once tanned and fresh, and the contours of her face recalled the lines of finely hewn soapstone. I noticed then how straight were her teeth, and that her small-breasted frame perfectly suited her irrepressible youth. She pushed the door open with girlish excitement before I could reach the handle.

"Have you heard from the bride?" I asked, getting in.

"Last night no more than ten times!"

"Is there a problem?"

"There's always a problem! You know Elizabeth!"

The truth is, I never really knew Elizabeth. Athena and Elizabeth were the daughters of Bishop and Mrs. Robert Van Fleet. They grew up in the Bishop's House on the far side of our garden wall, and as the only other residents of a city block of lawn, we pretended a familiarity that neither of us had known.

Athena and Elizabeth attended the Episcopal girls' school, and though I was a student at its male counterpart, most of my contact with the Van Fleet girls was through the bare whispers and distant rumors that bind such societies together. There had always been rumors about the Van Fleet girls—not only because they were striking examples of charismatic girlhood, but because their father was a bishop. And rumors couldn't help but abound around an office that remained the last remnant of British royalty in America.

Unlike our house, which fronted on the street, the Bishop's House faced away from public thoroughfares and overlooked the sanctuary we shared. I remember many warm summer nights when I sat alone on the garden wall, watching the nannies rocking two skinny-legged girls in the silent evening and shadows cast by the towering ionic columns of the great front porch. I longed for more than a neighborly wave or a chance passing on Arrow Street, but when they were not in school, or playing field hockey until 6 o'clock, they were being whisked off to art school or birthday parties in a black driven car.

In a time when our house stood too silent for a boy, I couldn't help but envy the magic I imagined went on inside that place. I walked past its gate every day to and from school, surreptitiously stealing a sidelong glance into the private courtyard. A fruit man came twice a week in an age when there was no longer such a thing; there was always a stream of cooks and caterers parading in and out of the service entrance; and on Saturday evenings, the circular drive was frequently filled with limousines from New York and Connecticut, as the grand house brimmed with butter-light.

Vietnam hadn't happened yet, Martin Luther King was a distant rumor, and President Kennedy, the handsome, smiling monarch of the right and just order of things. Whether it was just that insular place, or that fleeting time of life when all that matters ends just up the street, I'll never know. For what boy could tell the beat of the world from the beat of his hopeful heart?

Though this was the world from which we had come, it was not the world where I was going. Yale had been a holdover too of old-world theocracy—of libraries and colleges and civilized silence through the shaded heat of high noon—but shaken as it was by the tumultuous sixties, it had been changed forever. Gone were notions of principle and truth; gone, the idea of the good; gone, the brilliant scholarship boys in their little dusty rooms. In their stead was the illustrious marketplace, to be ruled by the business boys, in suspenders, school ties, and pocket watch fobs, forged in very new gold.

This may have been what the two of us shared in those intervening years—the passing of a world our peers had never known, and disappointment at what had arrived. Though never confessed, we presumed a way of the world that our friends had not. It was as if we expected that life could be lived on the bet that there was a God, which bestowed a world of beauty and grace to those who were granted its secrets.

I will never forget the pregnant pause as we drove past the gates of Rosecliff. There it sat for the world to behold, a bastion of magnificence, glimmering between the water and a deep green lawn along Bellevue Avenue. Breaking her own significant silence—as though she had seen an end—she exclaimed, "If I could live in any house in the world, it would be that one!"

"You know it's for sale."

Athena laughed. "Do you have five million I can borrow?"

"I'll leave that to Ted."

"He says houses are a bad investment."

"What do you say?"

"That romance is the only investment worth making!"

"And?" I provocatively asked.

She smiled through the windshield. "Ted's about as romantic as a tennis racket."

No one bought houses on Bellevue anymore. Few could afford to buy them, and still fewer could afford the style of life that was required to fill them. So, beginning in the sixties, as each estate was abandoned for modern life, the Preservation Society would snatch it up, and its former occupants squeeze into a twenty-room dwelling just off the drive.

Rosecliff was not the grandest of the mansions. And this was part of its charisma. On a street that held dream after dream of nineteenth-century robber barons, who had come to believe in their monarchies in an unfortunately democratic state, its graceful restraint in the company of The Breakers and Marble House, allowed it a presence that didn't have to prove its preeminence.

Maybe it was its understated facade that attracted so flamboyant a past. Rosecliff was designed in 1898 by the notorious Stanford White—the womanizing architect of some of the most prominent landmarks in America. Shot by a jealous husband while at lunch on a rooftop garden in New York, he was a sobering reminder of the treachery of beauty at any cost.

It was fashioned after the 'Little Palace' in the gardens of Versailles. In lieu of pink marble, the mansion was constructed of brilliant terracotta, which radiated in the day and held the sun into the cool of the summer evenings. A stately bank of Palladian windows stretched across the front of the house, holding in its frame a hundred-foot ballroom and three thousand miles of ocean.

After years of neglect, the once magnificent gardens looked worn and shapeless. But the discerning eye could see how they had once held an explosion of sculpted green and roses. Whether the house made the proprietor, or the proprietor made the house, for half a century Rosecliff stood as a vision of immortality.

It was said of its first mistress, Mrs. Morrison Bamberger, wife of Adolph Bamberger, the Philadelphia coal magnate, that in her first day of residence she lined up a platoon of gardeners in the ballroom, and with her own strong foot, rolled out an oriental carpet and demanded, "Reproduce it!" The next proprietress, Mrs. Jameson Whitney, gave the dazzling parties that made Rosecliff the preeminent venue of the 1920s. When the Navy declined the small fortune she offered to anchor the fleet out on the water, she allegedly hired every boat within twenty miles of coastline to don ten thousand lights and moor out in the dark as a mock flotilla.

For all its grandeur, which by the 1980s verged on parody, its deceptive human scale intimated a house that could be lived in. As fed up as I was with my own excesses, I nonetheless had to admit that if I were sentenced to a royal life, the prison I would choose was Rosecliff. Before I could agree with my romantic companion, she enthusiastically proclaimed, "It has that lovely little cottage just inside the gate—where Elizabeth could live!"

"Your house is big enough for ten sisters," I said.

"Ted won't have it," she said.

"Why not?" I pursued her.

"He says he won't have anyone who's 'slow' living under his roof."

It was the kind of remark I came to expect of the illustrious Ted Talbot. The truth is, I didn't understand how Athena came to be with Ted in the first place. I only knew that they met at Columbia, where Ted had won a tennis scholarship, and that before his junior year he joined the international circuit and was winning several million a year.

Athena had gone with him, and by the time they arrived at Wimbledon, the sports world was reading about their marriage in the papers. However wary I may have been about the 'Go-Go 80s', I have to admit I was as spellbound by fame as the rest of my generation. Still, given Ted's intolerance of the slightest sign of weakness, I found myself wondering if Ted himself may have been a bit 'slow'.

Elizabeth Van Fleet was anything but slow. She was a gifted child in a world that uses the term too liberally. At the age of twelve, she had given her first piano recital at Brown, and a year later, two of her paintings were hung in the Boston Children's Museum.

One knew at a glance that Athena and Elizabeth had to have been sisters. Elizabeth's face was blessed with the same striking symmetry, the same unconscious grace. But she was a rarefied version of Athena—her long straight hair, regally pulled back against her temples, and her dress, simple and elegant as though she were about to step onto a concert stage.

Unlike Athena's, Elizabeth's eyes didn't laugh at the corners, but peered into the distance as if they were looking for something very far away. It was nothing less than a beautiful face, retaining the features of her sister, but with a whisper of sadness that made one want to paint her. If Athena was the American girl at her finest, Elizabeth was a Netherlands princess.

I remember them best in July, after finishing school and before their August weeks on Block Island, running down the broad sloping lawn in tattered cotton dresses. They were startling girls of summer celebration at a time when such innocence had passed, laughing and falling and swinging and dreaming beneath the great oak trees. As I watched them through the garden gate, I realized there was a love they shared that would never be broken—that in the end, after all the bickering and cat-clawing and envy, nothing can come between sisters.

At the tender age of fifteen, gifted, sensitive girls either grow into women or they snap. If, for daughters, fathers are the gods that never die, I wondered what it must have been like to watch one die as a bishop. Not that there were many poor misguided souls around who still believed that by being a bishop, a man was closer to being God; but on the other hand, there weren't many poor misguided souls who didn't.

Assuming that God is a tall, handsome, craggy-faced Anglican, Robert Van Fleet looked like God. And when he died so suddenly that spring, the world across the garden wall came crashing in. No more than a week had passed when Henry Walsh, a trustee of the Diocese, appeared at the door of the Bishop's House with his upstanding teenage son.

I knew it to be Mr. Walsh because Henry Jr. was a classmate of mine. A celebrated athlete, he had found further notoriety in our senior year as the lucky choice of Athena. As I walked past the gate on Arrow Street, I imagined their visit to be a late condolence or tidings of a college acceptance.

On my return, I heard a gunshot resound across the courtyard. At first, I wasn't sure what it was—before I saw a kilted school girl running down the lawn from the house with a pistol in her hand. I charged across the driveway and up the steps to see young Henry on the foyer floor, clutching his leg and screaming in a way any self-respecting boy would regret.

The Walshes hadn't come on a social visit. Henry Sr. was there to convey the terms of their departure—they were to leave by summer's end when the new bishop was elected. His final punctuation was that Henry Jr. would no longer be seeing Athena; circumstances had 'changed', he said, and after all, they would soon be parting for college.

All this came out at the hearing, and that in the middle of the dark exchange, Elizabeth disappeared into the butler's pantry and returned with a loaded handgun kept in the event of an intruder. They never found the gun, and Elizabeth was committed to an institution. Her refusal to utter a word on the stand was taken as an admission of insanity, and after their last days following the judgment, the sisters were separated.

As the end drew near, I lingered long into the evenings along the garden wall. It may have been my way of saying goodbye to my lifelong neighbors, or perhaps of mourning the impending loss of what had been a magnificent world. The Kennedys were gone with my adolescence, the gun-runners had taken over, and the unrequited loves of skinny young boys, dismissed as a naive past.

It was on the eve of Elizabeth's leave-taking that I heard one of the girls crying. I climbed the wall to see it was Athena, weeping before the old oak swing. "I know!" she sobbed to her gently rocking sister. "I know you did it for me!" She held her sister's face in her hands. "But you didn't have to do it!" Athena pleaded. "You didn't have to do it! You didn't!"

Elizabeth sat slumped in the swaying swing, staring lifelessly at the ground. As Athena's anguish yielded to tears, I realized Elizabeth was singing. I wouldn't have

remembered the song, except that she sang it over and over
again—to her sister, and to me, and to the falling night:

    Love goes
    Round like a circle
    And comes back a knockin'
    At your front door.
    Love goes
    Round like a circle
    And comes back a knockin'
    At your front door.

Chapter 2

Except for an occasional passing reference to Athena on the sports page, I heard nothing more of the Van Fleet girls for the next ten years. It was then the rumor rolled through Newport that the infamous Ted Talbot had left the international circuit and bought the Cornwallace property on the Neck. Forced to retire at the age of thirty-one with chronic tendinitis, he had taken his fortune to be the youngest-ever President of the Tennis Hall of Fame.

I had just completed my first free-lance job when I got wind of their impending arrival. Before leaving Paris, I had sent a query to Wooden Boat Magazine, and thanks to a contact and three writing samples, I had a job to return to. I already felt at home in my house, the town, and my American life, rising at six and writing till noon in the back of the living room.

And it offered me a chance to assess anew the family legacy. As easy as it was to track the Adams after the Revolution—of money, power, and lauded names carved in too many stones—there was a dank reality, drifting through the rooms that I remembered as a child, and which, for the first time in our glorified past, suggested we might even be human. Perhaps I was searching for a greater life beyond the one I was living, a more compelling vocation than the alibi of work that brought me back to Newport.

My aunt would have called it a 'busman's holiday', whose agreeable assignments provided my excuse for self-indulgent reflection. As humid as it was that spring, with bare feet sticking to the floors, I chased the traces of my family's past like a relentless genealogist. I happily read and wandered about, taking down old leather books—until I opened a sea captain's chest that was as closed as Pandora's box.

When I came upon the slave trading ledger and realized what it was, I anxiously scanned it for as long as I could, then returned it to the chest. As oblivious as I had managed to be throughout my entitled life, on the cusp of turning thirty, whence I'd come could no longer be ignored. The past was no longer a happy legacy of Yankee ingenuity—romanticized by terms like 'Triangle Trade' and visions of the wide-open sea—but ships of human beings, stolen from their homes and African identities, to be enslaved as 'Henry', 'Polly', and 'Matilda', in the service of my family.

Averting my eyes from these inconvenient facts and family embarrassments, I conveniently turned my attention to the Talbots and went over to welcome them. Since Athena and I had never been more than childhood acquaintances, I anticipated a stilted, if not disingenuous, reunion. But I was immediately put at ease by her generous memory—recognizing me before I was able to close the door of my car.

"Brooke Adams?" she called, from the depth of the garden. "Brooke! Could that be you?" Shedding her gloves, she ran over and threw her arms around me like a long-lost friend. "What are you doing here?" she gushed.

"I live here," I said.

Beguilingly, she laughed. She hadn't lost her perpetually smiling face, and the features of her youth had refined with the grace of having become a woman.

"Then I *do* have a friend in Newport!" she said, embracing me again. "Come in!" she effervesced, taking my hand. "You have to meet my partner in crime!"

The house sat atop a gentle rise, overlooking the ocean. It was a big timber-framed summer place that had been winterized several years before. A house that could have been designed by Frank Lloyd Wright in his early days, with long sweeping roofs projecting in all directions; massive chimneys rising on every pitch; and an exterior of weathered shakes and diamond-leaded windows.

The enormous varnished entry shone in the long cool shadows of the morning. We walked back together to the rear of the house, and Athena stopped at a doorway. In the middle of the room, a fit young man clad in tennis whites was standing over an expansive desk, studying a magazine.

"Ted," Athena called, "I want you to meet my childhood sweetheart—Brooke Adams!"

He was shorter than one would have postulated by the magic of the television screen. With the exception of a disproportionately developed right arm, he looked too lean to be a champion. He lingered over his reading for another moment, then broke away and made his way across the room.

"From childhood!" His husky voice gave the impression he had shouted at one too many tennis matches.

"Watch out for a man who comes before your time! How the hell are ya', Brooke?"

He extended the powerful arm in my direction, and his hand convincingly gripped mine. I wondered what it must have been like to be Ted Talbot's tennis racket.

"Put on a few pounds since college, have ya', Brooke? Gotta get you out on the courts!" The truth is, I had always been underweight—I suspected he had used the line before. "Must be the glasses," he deliberated. "For some goddam reason, no one with glasses is ever any good at tennis."

Surveying me with his quick, dark eyes, which habitually looked away, he telegraphed an impulsiveness that made me mistrust his intentions. He had a small, sharp nose and a tight, angry mouth that would twist to a sardonic sneer, and his closely shaved scalp of ink-black hair crested to a little flip. He reminded me of the perennial adolescent who terrorized every weak boy in school, luring his prey with a cordial hand into an ingratiating chance to shake it— then prematurely withdrawing the offer in ridicule of such trust, with a cynical grin that defied every naïve victim he came across.

Ted Talbot wasn't nicknamed 'Tizzy' by accident or happenstance. In a sport that had long been the private property of genteel society, Ted was the first to show the sport could appeal to baser instincts. He became known for his sudden outbursts of anger, throwing rackets at unsuspecting fans, and after an unfavorable call at Forest Hills, toppling an umpire from his towering chair.

"Welcome to my place," he introduced himself, with evident satisfaction.

"It's a nice house," I agreed.

He strolled to a rear window and plunged his hands into his tennis shorts. "It will be once we get that done," he lamented, as if suffering a grave injustice. I followed him to the window, where bulldozers were moving mounds of earth on the lawn.

"Believe it or not, that was once a court, but it had more weeds than Athena's garden!" He pondered this a moment. "Now we'll have the grass and a championship clay."

I nodded, as knowingly as I could. He turned and slapped me firmly on the back. "Come over and play anytime, Brooke! Better yet, give me your number!"

Going back to his desk, he picked up a pen. As I recited the number, I couldn't help noticing the magazines on the blotter. The one he had been reading was a catalog, "Drug Runner's Clearinghouse: Their Loss is Your Gain," boasting cover photographs of a Porsche, a contemporary glass house on a cliff, and a phallic speedboat skimming through the water.

Two periodicals next to it bore identical silhouettes of a bearded man with a screw through his head. One was titled, "Techniques of Harassment: How the Underdog Gets Even," and the second, "Harassment Continued: The Poor Man's Justice by Telephone."

"Ted's educational reading!"

I turned to see Athena in the doorway.

"It's more than I learned at Columbia!" he said.

She laughed. "You may be right!"

"The world is my classroom," Ted pronounced. "I study the book of life!"

"Which life is that?" Athena retorted, ironically grinning at me.

"The only one worth living!" he said. "Survival of the fittest!"

On that note, I sensed it was time to go and went over to shake his hand. Behind him, I noted a soaring wall festooned with big game trophies.

"Are you the hunter?" I asked.

"What else is there to do when you're not playing tennis?"

Ted disappeared into another room, and I walked through the entry with Athena.

"It was different…wasn't it?" Athena mused, leaning against the front door.

"What was different?"

"The world," she said.

"Which one?"

"The one in Providence."

"Yes," I said. "It was different."

"Was it as good as I remember?"

"What do you remember?"

"The garden. The house. A time when the world was one."

"Yes," I said. "It was as good."

"Was it our age? Or the time?"

"What's the difference?" I glibly replied.

She smiled. "There is no difference."

With that, she came forward and kissed me on the cheek. "You bring it back, Brooke Adams," she said. "You bring it back to me."

I saw the two of them a good deal after that. Athena and I spent many golden afternoons in the solarium, kindling memories and recalling a friendship that probably never was. And Ted decided I possessed the two qualities he most admired—that I had a lot of money, and thanks to our unromantic past, that I didn't love Athena.

"Why did you move to Paris?" she asked from her loveseat one golden afternoon.

Challenging her inquisitive eyes, I said, "I had no place else to go."

She stared at me for a long, drawn-out moment, then threw back her head and laughed. Her white teeth flashed in the strong sea sun, her youthful neck arched and her dark hair shone, and her small, tanned breasts were pressed like a girl's beneath a sheer silk blouse. "If ever I have no place else to go," she exclaimed, "it might as well be Paris!

"Were you in love?" she asked at last.

"Many times," I said.

"With whom?" she unexpectedly pried.

I remember being taken aback. "With every beautiful woman," I said, "that I passed on the Champs-Élysées."

Her laughter splashed again—as though she had been waiting fifteen years to laugh—a full, free laugh that could only have come from so supple a throat as hers. "The trouble with you, Brooke Adams," she said, "is that you don't have enough faith!"

"I have faith!" I defended myself.

"You do?" she skeptically intoned. "Enough to believe there is only one woman in the world you were destined to love?"

"Maybe—not quite enough," I allowed.

She enigmatically gazed.

"Do you?" I asked.

"Do I what?"

"Have enough faith?" I said.

She grinned. "Yes!"

"I envy you," I said.

"For being married to Ted?"

"For believing in destiny," I said.

She quizzically fixed on me. "The sixties were hard for you, weren't they, Brooke?"

I had never thought about it. "Maybe," I conceded.

"How?" she inquired.

"They must have been…too cynical for me."

"Too cynical for *you*?" she sarcastically came back.

"Somehow—I felt betrayed."

"By whom?" she asked.

"Maybe—by my family. Probably by the time."

"So, you escaped to Paris!" she instantly rejoiced. "Did you find what you were looking for?"

"Not yet," I said. "What about you?"

She whimsically smiled. "Not yet."

That year, I asked myself many times what had drawn Athena to Ted. I never wondered for a minute what attracted Ted to Athena. Bullish, conceited men survive their insecurities by tying themselves to beautiful women.

Yet, Athena was so much more than that. What I knew in my private encounters with her, I had witnessed as much in public. At the first Newport party we attended together, I watched her hypnotize a host of swooning suitors, young and old, married and unattached, enchant and cajole and fascinate them, then leave with Ted before midnight.

"You buy money, Mr. Crawford?" she asked. "Isn't that like selling advertising?"

"Perhaps," Crawford said, starry-eyed. "Though I'm not exactly sure what you mean."

"Or insuring insurance companies," Athena said. "Why would anyone do that?"

"They're all fine professions," Crawford declared. "I'd love you to see the bank."

"Thank you, Mr. Crawford," she wryly replied, "but I'll be busy talking to myself."

For this was the lost age after the wars, when our only enemy was that there was none, and the only victory to be won was the private possession of power. Money, prestige, some sign of success was all that we came to crave, and the fight for freedom, and justice, and hope, lay in a soldier's grave. However pathetic we may have seemed to old men worn by the wars, we had donned adulthood at too young an age in order to make heroes again. I wondered if Athena was as lost as I in those empty, ensuing years—and too restless for brokers and bondsmen and banks, said yes to a traveling man.

Chapter 3

It was only a week before flying north in Athena's Aston Martin that I was invited to attend Elizabeth's wedding in Ashfield, Massachusetts. The Crawfords were having their May Day party, and never having gone, I went—only to watch the maypole standing deserted in the setting sun.

"Look at it, Connie," I heard Crawford say, "no one is dancing—it's limp! Maybe you should go up to the kitchen and rustle out some of the help!"

Wanting to avoid Crawford's recruitment, I started down toward the bay, where I came upon Athena at the edge of the pool, crying into her wine. She was wearing a peach-tinged, double-breasted dress, pleated from a dropped waist, inspiring me to think no flapper from the twenties could have rivaled Athena Van Fleet. Ted leered at me from the library as I passed through the house to the garden—encircled by a smoking club of would-be athletes, had arthritis not set in.

When she saw me, she furtively wiped her eyes and forced an unconvincing smile. The linen lapels were pressed against her chest, and flecked with bittersweet tears.

"Are you alright?" I asked her.

She sighed, "I'm—alright."

"Is there anything I can do?"

"There's nothing—anyone can do," she said.

I stood there, feeling helpless.

"Actually," she impulsively came back, "would you come to Elizabeth's wedding?"

"Elizabeth's—wedding?"

"Ted can't come. Would you come with me?"

"Are you sure?" I asked.

"It would mean a lot. It would mean a lot to me."

"I'd be happy to," I gladly accepted.

"It would mean a lot to me."

Winging our way to Ashfield, Massachusetts in the slipstream of that moment, as she raced through the gears, I considered this restless American girl at my side. It was not that she hailed from colonial stock that had arrived at Plymouth Rock. Whatever may have been the Van Fleet lineage—perhaps born from the loins of a scullery maid and those of a Netherlands prince—she seemed instinctively free of the tyranny of my own ancestral England, giving me to think the greatest aristocracy of all was never having had one.

As she stared through the windshield, I noted how rarely she engaged the world with her eyes. She seemed perpetually distracted—as though she were remembering another place or time—as though she were recalling a world we did not, or were too apathetic to remember. If Athena embodied the American girl in all her spontaneity, she held fast to a past that somehow looked ahead, as one who was already beyond us.

"Brooke, you're wonderful for coming!" she said. "And you look great in a khaki suit!"

"I hope it's formal enough," I replied.

"I told you not to dress."

"It's a wedding!" I protested.

Athena laughed. "Like none you've ever seen!"

"How is it Elizabeth is marrying a farmer?"

"She's desperate to get out of the home. Her only way out is to get married," she said.

"Or for you to take her in?"

"For *us* to take her in—which Ted will never do."

"Never?" I gratuitously asked.

"'Never' is Ted's middle name."

My superior aunt would have written Ted off as a case of inferior breeding. As often as she managed to miss the point, she had an uncanny gift for coming up with all the right answers for all the wrong reasons. There was something missing in a man like Ted, for all his talent and advantage, which gave me to fear if he were given free rein, the world was headed for trouble.

"Will Elizabeth ever be happy again?"

"If she can forget the past."

"How can you forget the past?"

Athena smiled. "You can't."

Ashfield was one of those New England towns one often reads about and never sees—exuding the myth of a time-lost life, long since taken by the grind and ambition of twentieth-century America. When we arrived, people were filtering into the white church on the common. Topped by a leaning steeple, it was a diminutive wooden structure, which would have looked humble if not for a fresh coat of paint that allowed it quiet pride.

The bell was ringing when we got out of the car. As we approached, a small elderly man in an acolyte's robe appeared on the stoop with a crucifer's cross, smoking a cigarette. As a last congregant passed through the door, he was waving his arms at us. "Hurry! Hurry! Da' pestibal beginnin'! Da' weddin' pestibal beginnin'!"

The church smelled like the rain had gotten in. We sidled past several lingering guests and stopped in the middle of the narthex. There, at the foot of the carpeted aisle, stood Elizabeth Van Fleet.

She was tall, even taller than her graceful gown claimed, and as lithe as she had been as a girl. Her gaunt cheeks bore the telltale signs of Athena's unassuming beauty—but something in her countenance had changed. I wasn't sure if it was due to what I knew about her past, or what ten years in an institution must have taken from her; what I knew was, for all her undeniable grace, Elizabeth had changed.

It was not that she was no longer beautiful—she continued to be a striking example of aristocratic presentation. It was that every aura of her youth was gone. There was a sternness in her brow, a blankness in her gaze, which would allow one to believe she'd shot a man.

"Attie!" she cried, and dropping her bouquet, lunged through the crowd with outstretched arms. They embraced for a long moment, and it was then the tenderness returned to her face. But when they parted it was gone, and I was left to recall how, in spite of it all, together they had forged an inviolable covenant that would never be broken.

One expects a comical assembly of relations at any accident of marriage, but this was more pronounced than the usual case. The nave was studded with diamonds, sparkling from the ears of familiar-looking ladies I vaguely recognized from Providence. Between these scattered niches of elegance were enclaves of worn-looking figures, swaying unpredictably in the pews like branches in the wind.

As we approached the last empty pew just beneath the pulpit, a young man fell sideways into the aisle and landed at my feet. He proceeded to yawn from the instant his head thumped the carpeted floor, to the time I concluded no damage had been done and had gotten him back up again. I wondered what Athena must have been thinking behind her inscrutable grin—observing what scarcely qualified as a bona fide Episcopal church—but as the self-possessed daughter of a bishop, she carried it off like a sovereign, comporting herself with the confidence of one who had never known self-doubt.

There began a wheezing sound, and then a sharp clatter, as the little organ on the side wall commenced to play, 'The Wedding March'. The organist, who looked like a retired English tutor from St. Paul's, began to audibly grunt over the calliopeic melody blowing from the pipes. His feet fumbled from pedal to pedal in socks, and I deduced that his approximate style of play was due to a withered right arm.

The congregation rose and turned to the rear in expectation of Elizabeth's entrance. The groom and best man, in stiffly pressed tuxedoes, came through a door behind the altar on tentative steps that carried them together in time to the center aisle. As the groom surveyed his stunning intended, advancing toward the front, I thought how he managed to successfully mimic a very natty chimney sweep.

Athena's eyes were fixed on her breathtaking sister when the priest appeared. The moment Elizabeth arrived at the railing, the music abruptly stopped. As we sat down together, he traversed the chancel and climbed into the pulpit.

The most useful advice my aunt ever gave me had to do with making judgments. "Brooke," she said, "whatever it is, always trust your first impression." Despite my inclination to do otherwise, I have taken this to heart. So, from the moment he appeared on that horizon which keeps us from those we'll never meet—that distressing boundary which binds us from possibilities we'll never know—I felt as if his fortuitous arrival was no less than an ordained encounter, on an unfolding landscape of my destiny, and the truth of my unanchored life.

If the capacity to hope is the sole measure of what it means to be a man, he was everything a man could be. Scanning the crowd as though his life had been brought to one desperate moment—when he would find or not the elusive satisfaction of all he was born to be—it was in his shining eyes, searching back and forth across the congregation, in search of some unfathomable future, or something he had lost. Though it was the sort of hope one instantly knew could never be fulfilled, it was the sort that was worth the chance it gave to glimpse the limits of human longing.

In retrospect, his face was indefinably handsome: deep-set eyes, a forehead like a shelf, a disarmingly engaging smile. But it wouldn't be until I watched him navigate the mean streets of our time that I came to recognize his exaggerated features as no less than magnificent. Distracted as I was by this lanky cleric, barely filling out his suit, I didn't notice my companion, unexpectedly agog. "My God, that's John Pickett!"

The priest's eyes instantly fell to our pew and lighted on Athena. His lips began to quiver, and sweat beaded on his brow. The flush of his face was gone.

The rest of the service was a veritable liturgy of nervousness, in which he dropped the wedding rings, twice lost his place in the Prayer Book, and his voice more times than that. As Elizabeth's train disappeared into the narthex, Athena was tugging on my sleeve. "Come, Brooke," she said, staring down the aisle, "I have to see—you need to meet John Pickett!"

She peered at me and smiled, before cocking her head, as if to ask why I would hesitate. I shrugged, and then she laughed and squeezed me on the cheek—to say that I was jealous—and if I didn't love her, I pitied those who did, save the man who found his love returned. As she gazed at me, and stretched her slender neck from her silk lemon dress and string of pearls, she made me feel that anything was possible in love, except the chance that it might not be so.

Athena went ahead through the milling crowd, making inquiries as she went. She turned around and motioned to a narrow staircase that ascended just inside the front door. Navigating the narthex, I followed her up the stairs to the top, where I had to look around her elevated shoulder for my second inspection of the priest.

"John Pickett?" I heard her breathlessly exclaim. "Is that—really you?"

He was kissing his stole as he looked up, and helplessly stared at Athena. It was one of those stares which might give one to think that he had never seen her before. And then, when it went on, however fancifully, that he had seen her all his life.

"You're not skinny anymore!" she said.

It was then he smiled, and his restless fidgeting, reminiscent of a nervous acolyte, unaccountably gave way to a startling visage of conviction.

"I'm glad to see you again," he said. He said it in a way that made me feel like every truth I thought I'd told was a lie. It was a smile that I guessed could not have been passed down by the accident of parents, but by some wrinkle in the universe where changelings and dreamers lay hid from the visible world.

"And your clothes fit!" she said.

He bashfully looked down and scrutinized his clerical suit. "I guess I'm not skinny anymore," he said.

Athena laughed with enchantment. "When did you start wearing Brooks Brothers suits?"

He smiled. "When I became a priest."

"I didn't know we paid you enough!" she said.

He blushed. "I'm paid too much."

Athena's mouth twitched with a momentary smile. She began to gaze at the tall, compelling priest, standing youthfully before her. As Pickett looked back through the pregnant silence—giving me to doubt that I was there—I turned and quietly started down the stairs, feeling like an intruder.

"Brooke," Athena called across her silken shoulder. "Could you take my car to the reception?" Tendering the keys, she contritely imparted, "I think I'll go with Father Pickett."

The elderly acolyte who heralded us in was stationed on the front step of the church. He was leaning on his crucifer's cross with a cigarette dangling from his mouth, handing out squares of construction paper with directions to the reception.

"Ya' made it!" he howled. Giggling with delight, he banged the cross on the step. "What d'ja tink ob da' pestibal?"

"I'll never forget it," I said.

"He tumtin', ain't he?"

"The groom?" I asked.

"Poh Crite' take, Padduh Pickett!"

Exploiting the opportunity, I asked, "Has he been here long?"

"One year, teben munt!" he replied. "Bet preet dit ole church eber had! 'Xcept por one ting," he cautioned. "'Pends too much time on peoples in town who nebba be comin' ta church! I tell him, I know dey be libin' in da' goddam woods, but dey ain't nebba be comin' ta church! But Paddah Pickett tays, dat don't matta' a wit—dey no dipperent prom you oh me!"

With that, he offered his wrinkled hand, and introduced himself as "Gordon." Thanking him for the reception directions, I bade him a definitive farewell.

"I'll tee ya' ober der!" Gordon guffawed. "Ya' ain't heard da' lat ob me!"

The hotel sat in the middle of a farmer's field within earshot of the highway. Its architecture was a remarkable blend of English Tudor and Feudal Castle, boasting a façade of stucco and timber, finished by twin stone turrets. Beneath a tremendous illuminated sign announcing "The Medieval

Manor," was the relevant postscript, "Goodbye Miss Van Fleet, Welcome Mrs. Hicks!"

I found 'Round Table Room, Side A' per my instructions, and passed a pair of studded wooden doors. Though no round table was in sight, the room was clearly set up for a reception. A long narrow table was elevated at the front and covered with a pink paper tablecloth; while ranks of smaller tables were deliberately angled in military flight formation.

Flanking the head table, what appeared to be a rock and roll band was setting up. One member was plugging in a high-voltage piano, while another was deliberately piecing together an impressive array of drums. A third musician, blowing into a microphone, was successfully producing shrill electronic pitches into the hall.

By his assertive gestures, I guessed the latter was the leader of the band. His beard was meticulously clipped, and he wore a rakish white suit and ruffled shirt unbuttoned to the waist. Crowning the ensemble, a large gold medallion lay entangled in the hairs of his chest.

The room was almost full, and the bridal party lined up at the door when Athena appeared. Seeing me, she gracefully swept through the crowd with Pickett right behind her. "You disappeared!" she ventured an apology, "before I could introduce you!"

Pickett graciously extended his hand, with no less than a dazzling smile. "I'm glad to meet you, Brooke," he said. "Athena is quite a fan!"

If ever I had met a satisfied man, it was then. If ever I had sensed a life fulfilled, if ever I had glimpsed a consummated hope, if ever I had seen a realized dream, it was in this tall, inexplicable priest, standing there before me. It was not the kind of satisfaction that comes from having earned it; it was the kind that comes as an unqualified gift from a God that was smiling down on him.

Scrutinizing Pickett's long, elegant nose, I was shamefully struck by how unintelligent I had found Ted Talbot's. As embarrassed as I was by such comparisons—at the inevitable expense of the victim—being that they were irrepressible, there was little I could do about it. So, I was moved to think how his white linen collar made him look almost gorgeous.

The band leader began to breathe heavily into the microphone, "Ladies and gentlemen, nhnhnh…it is time now, nhnhnh…to introduce, nhnhnh…the bridal party…"

"Brooke, we're being summoned!" Athena said, taking Pickett's hand.

As I watched them wend their way to the elevated table, I instinctively feared for them both. It was not that it was an inauspicious script, however true this happened to be. It was that I sensed a foreign enemy that posed a clear and present danger; yet what I didn't sense was that the foreign enemy was none other than ourselves.

I realized how suspicious of the church I had become. I wondered if it was that I continued to blame it for the death of my missioning parents. But it seemed like the suspicion of a whole generation, which grew up to resent an institution that was at best the guardian of bygone days, and at worst, a colossal waste of time.

There was something about every minister I'd known which led me to believe that, however worldly they may have appeared, they knew little about the world around them. It was not that they were ethereal, but that they'd given up on their hopes, and so trudged through life in black baggy suits, ignorant of the longings of men. Yet I knew at once—even at the height of his liturgical slips—that Pickett, for all his otherworldliness, was utterly worldly and different.

I thought how he possessed the poise of an Englishman and the passion of an American. His finely tailored suit, and starched white clerical collar ringing his neck, belied the impossible energy of youth which is peculiar to this continent. In every gesture, every nod, every tightening of his lips to accomplish what he hoped for in his life, one felt the earth's chaotic forces being pressed into the palm of his hand.

"Ladies and gentlemen, the parents of the groom—Charles and Candy Hicks!"

The crowd was applauding as the Hicks appeared and started down the aisle to their table. Mrs. Hicks was wearing a low-cut gown of purple polyester chiffon, blooming from the waist and over her hips with razor-edge precision. Mr. Hicks came limping along behind in a morning coat and tails—bringing with him a cane and the telltale thump of a low-tech wooden leg.

The ushers that followed in black tuxedos resembled a Sicilian crime family, while their escorts looked to have been selected for their uniformly oversized bosoms. As the band began to play *Love, Soft as an Easy Chair,* Elizabeth emerged with her new husband. Following her lead, the groom gingerly proceeded—as though he'd accidentally found himself on top of a wedding cake.

"Shame 'bout Charlie," a voice broke from behind.

I turned around to see that it was Gordon. The aged crucifer was leaning on his cross, still clad in his acolyte's robe.

"Lot' it in a tractor."

"Lost what?" I asked.

"Hid leg, por Crite take! Like da' band?"

I attempted a nod.

"Nuttin' like my band."

"You have a band?" I inquired.

"'Til we 'plit up. Now I ain't got no more drinkin' money," he lamented.

"Where did you play?"

"Up da' road! Ashpield Inn," he explained. "I beat da' bongo, an' my buddied played piano an' guitar. But den we plit up."

"I'm sorry to hear it."

"Tickt buckt a night por each ob us," he said. "Now no more. No more drinkin' money. Gotta go back ta' da' Big Top."

"You worked in the circus?"

"Clownin'," he said. "'Til da' tent caught pire in Hartpord."

The band leader breathed into the microphone again, instructing us to take our places. As I searched for my place card, Gordon followed, and when I finally found my chair, he gleefully plunked down in what was to have been Vicki Skorupski's seat. His wrinkled face was shrunken with delight—as if he knew something that I didn't.

"Did you come here after the circus?" I asked.

"Nope. Worked on da' railroad. 'Til dey got rid ob da' cabooted," he said.

I knowingly pursed my lips.

"Den dey 'topped worryin' 'bout railroad time. I detided, da' hell wid it. I detided, ya' don't gib a damn 'bout railroad time, ya' don't gib a damn 'bout me!"

It was a cash bar, and I asked if I could buy him a drink. He said I could buy him two, so I returned balancing a Scotch on the rocks and two double-Vodkas with no ice. Dinner had been served in my absence; I was sure it was chicken, though painstakingly rolled into the likeness of a regulation baseball.

A half-glass of champagne stood next to my plate, with a pink ribbon tied around the stem. There was a little mesh bag of candy-covered almonds, closed with a matching bow. Completing the ensemble was a white book of matches propped against the bag—inscribed with the exhortation, "Elizabeth and Charlie, The Perfect Match."

After dinner, the groom and his formidable mother were invited to the floor, and the band aptly struck up an unusual rendition of *The Way We Were*. The wedding cake was wheeled out—evoking a miniature Leaning Tower of Pisa—to scattered gasps of appreciation from the crowd. It was then that I noticed Athena and Pickett were gone from their appointed places.

When the dance was done, I turned to Gordon, excusing myself with a smile that implied an urgent trip to the men's room. On my way to the lobby, a family in swimsuits was headed for the pool, while, beyond a veil of tropical plants, another wedding was in progress. Beneath the lifeguard's chair, the freshly minted newlyweds were in a passionate embrace as a rotund, elderly gentleman dove into the water behind them.

I strolled around the parking lot, kicking broken glass and throwing stones into the open field. The grass on the hill behind the hotel was blowing in a gentle breeze, and on top of the rise, a windswept oak was holding the setting sun. It had been almost an hour when I grew impatient with Athena's disappearance, making rounds about the Aston Martin as if proximity might bring her back.

Just as I was beginning to regret having overlooked the newlyweds, Elizabeth and Charlie came charging out of the hotel through a spray of rice. I made my way across the parking lot as they approached the limousine. As though she had been expecting me, Elizabeth uncannily looked up— and without missing a beat, faintly smiled and replied, "Hello, Brooke."

I was startled that she recognized me.

Dismissing my hackneyed congratulations, she said, "Thank you for coming."

"My privilege," I said.

"Tell Athena that I love her."

"I'm not sure where she's gone."

"She's with Father Pickett," Elizabeth replied. Staring at me—with that look of honesty one often sees in the mentally unstable—her limpid eyes appeared stunningly distracted, as if by something in the distance. "The last time I saw you was at the shooting."

"I remember," I confessed.

"I wasn't crazy, you know. They all thought I was crazy. Even Athena thought I was crazy."

"Athena loves you," I said.

"But I wasn't," she said. "You know, Brooke—that I wasn't."

Feeling like an innocent bystander implicated at the scene of the crime, I nonetheless feared, however crazy she was, that Elizabeth might have been right.

"It doesn't matter," she solemnly declared. "What matters is who loves Athena."

"Ted, I would hope!" I feigned the obvious.

"He never loved Athena."

"He's her husband," I self-righteously came back.

"He's a tennis player," she said.

"Just like the other one," she blithely went on. "Only Pickett loves Athena."

"The—priest?" I incredulously asked.

"He has loved her for a very long time."

Watching the limousine dissolve in the dusk, I realized how unsettling this had been. It was as though that meeting with Elizabeth was an encounter with some stark raving truth, however distorted by her violent sensitivities and blindness of her youth. If I was already aware of Ted's voracious need to suck the oxygen from every room—dismissing anyone who didn't have a role to play in his ambitious plans—as another jealous man, I admit I was perplexed by how he could disregard Athena, at the risk of losing a woman that the world had no choice but to venerate.

But in the end, it was hate that made tennis players great—jealousy, pride, the intent to defeat—and I wondered what kind of narcissistic abuse he had heaped on his beautiful wife. Ted was a product of this affluent time, who, caught by the surprise of sudden wealth, was given to remember only success, and forget about eternal love. So, I had to wonder what Elizabeth meant that Pickett had always loved Athena, and to believe that before my time had run out, I was sure to come to know.

It wasn't much longer before I heard the cascade of laughter behind me. I turned around to see two silhouettes, limned by the setting sun. The figure in the lead came charging ahead with dangling shoes in her hand, and the man who followed, descended the hill on a long and graceful stride.

In this day and age, one couldn't help seeing something of a parody in Pickett. At first, I thought it was the contradiction of any youthful cleric, in a time when the church had at best become an anachronistic institution. Then I realized it was a paradox that had to do with Pickett himself—some spontaneous faith that, regardless of incidental religious commitment, would try anything, would go anywhere, for the sake of some greater desire.

Unfounded as it was, I ineffably sensed that he was always ahead of me—that he intuitively knew what I wanted to say before I managed to say it. But never did I feel he was stealing away an intuition that was mine, and only that it was sure to come to fruit because we held it in common. Maybe it was that he saw so far ahead that what he saw was no longer the future, harkening back to so distant a past that time no longer meant a thing.

"I'm sorry, Brooke!" Athena gasped. "A lot has happened in a decade!"

"And I apologize," Pickett entreated. "I'm afraid I lost all sense of time."

Athena laughed. "Don't tell my partner that! All he ever says is, 'Time is money'!"

"I'm no businessman," Pickett repented, tentatively glancing at her.

"No!" Athena ecstatically approved. "You'll always be a man of God!"

Pickett managed a smile—as if he were uncertain that this was a compliment. I sensed he was waiting for some clarification, but she left her intention in the dusk. With a timely lull in the conversation, and lights coming on in the hotel, I obliquely implied a late-evening commitment for which I had to return.

With a look of desperation creasing his brow, Pickett shoved his hands into his pockets. "If you'd like to stay longer, I could bring you home," he said, and kicked a stone across the pavement.

Athena laughed. "It's a three-hour drive!"

His eyes were dashed to the asphalt.

"I mean," she atoned with tenderness, "I really have to get back."

Searching for her keys, if not for a distraction, she asked, "Will we see you again?"

"If you ever need a priest!" he almost implored.

"I'll always need a priest!" she said.

Bidding him farewell, I shook Pickett's hand and retreated to the far side of the car. Athena peered at him for a last lingering moment before reluctantly getting in; and with her eyes straight ahead, perhaps against her will, she fired the Aston Martin to life. As we departed for the road, I furtively peered into my rearview mirror—and we left the tall, dark figure standing alone, his arm extended in the dusk.

We must have driven for half an hour before we spoke again. Gazing at the dashboard, aglow with reflections of some forgotten London evening, I thought how it had been one of those days which might as well have been a lifetime. And I thought of how a day becomes a lifetime by the story it holds.

"Where did you meet Pickett?" I asked at last.

"At college," she thoughtfully mused. "He lived next door to Ted."

"It's hard to imagine Ted and Pickett as neighbors."

She smiled. "They weren't."

"Has Pickett changed?" I asked.

"I'm not sure," she reflected. "I really don't remember much about him—except that he was handsome.

"Terrifically handsome," she wistfully sighed. "Handsome, and a scholarship student."

"That must have been a tricky combination," I said, as one who'd suffered neither financial uncertainty nor extraordinary good looks.

"More difficult for Ted," Athena said, smiling through the windshield. "He once insisted, when he was drunk, that Pickett was in love with me."

"What gave him that idea?"

"You know Ted. Every man's in love with me."

"Every man?" I teased.

"Every man but you. Which is why he likes you," she said.

However heroically I held at bay any romantic feelings for Athena, the truth is I found little consolation in this last playful remark. I'm not sure if it was my ego at stake—or if, for the first time I wanted her—what I knew was, there was something in those sparkling eyes, something in that perpetually laughing gaze of hers, which made me wish I was the only man she had ever cared about. But I knew it was no better founded a wish than that of the next waiting suitor, who would hope for the same thing on touching her hand, or basking in her perfection.

"He does have a way of falling all over himself when he's with me."

"When he's with you, or with any woman?"

Athena grinned. "With me."

As principled as I knew Athena to be, I was surprised by this flirtation. Yet, puzzled as I was by her relationship with Ted, I had begun to understand that Athena didn't fit anywhere in this world, and had to take whatever came along. Her life no longer knew the beauty or the grace—the harmonies of the garden wall—sung so sweetly through those precious, passing days of youth, and gone without a trace.

The fact is, I knew nothing of Athena's life since the day she left the Bishop's House. I typically presumed that in my absence, little of note could have happened. Yet now I wondered if she had learned not to grieve, and began to celebrate downtown—if only to express the unspeakable fear that nothing would bring happiness again.

"How did Ted decide that Elizabeth was crazy?"

"The way Ted decides anything."

"Elizabeth was always—sensitive," I tried.

"Brooke, you don't know the whole story."

Staring through the windshield, the car began to slow. "Henry tried to rape me the night before the shooting. Elizabeth saw it all."

Dumbfounded, I started: "Did he—"

"Of course not!" she laughed, and put her foot to the floor.

"What—happened?" I gasped, pressed back in my seat.

"Henry didn't walk for a week!"

At that moment, I wanted to laugh with her, but somehow I just couldn't. I'm not sure why, except that I knew the laughter wasn't what it appeared. It wasn't a cynical laughter, nor a laughter of sadness, but a laughter that hid something—somewhere behind that enchanting gaze, that captivating smile, that seemingly ultimate belief in herself as the grantor of the world's salvation.

Arriving in Newport, I heard the church bell ringing into the soft spring night, and roll across the glimmering lawns of Newport to the sea. For all its faults, the church had stood 250 years as the single constant in what had been a turbulent, mad town. And however suspicious I may have been of institutional religion, I was happy to know the historic tower was going to be restored.

Chapter 4

I didn't hear from Athena for several weeks when one morning I was roused out of bed by the phone. She and Ted were chairing the search for the new Episcopal rector, and asked if I would be willing to serve as the fifth member of the committee. The others were to be Leonard Madison, former treasurer of the church—who happened to be investment broker for half the portfolios in Newport—and Spencer Grayson, a currency speculator who would be away in Brussels.

"And guess who's coming tonight!" she exclaimed. Before I could surmise, she ecstatically interrupted, "Father Pickett!" I was to come to dinner at seven, where he'd be interviewed around the table.

I was already feeling uncomfortable before I put down the receiver. The prospect inspired the same sensation as betting at a second-rate horse track—the race was run before it had started, and win or lose, one knew it was won by the ill-gotten gains of another man's hand. Though the odds against his inexperience should have been unduly high, when Athena called to say his car had broken down, I eagerly set out for Ashfield.

I was to look for a big old country place on the hill behind the church. Pickett rented the carriage house, she said, but I should meet him down on the road. When I arrived, he wasn't there—though a tow truck was descending the gravel drive with a little French car on its haunches.

Pickett's calling card was tacked to the door. As I proceeded up the stairs, romantic visions of a pastoral equestrian life quickly gave way to the less than romantic pungency of horse manure. The door was ajar at the top of the stairs; peering inside, I saw two long legs crossed from behind a *Wall Street Journal*.

"Hello!" I called. The legs twitched in the chair, and the *Journal* somersaulted to the floor.

"Brooke!" Pickett started, immediately standing. "I was supposed to meet you down at the church! I'm—terribly sorry! You're early!"

"Then I'm the one to be sorry."

"Oh, no," he objected, "please—come in! You get to see my little—pied-à-terre!"

He wasn't wearing his clerical collar. An immaculately pressed linen jacket hung from his angular shoulders. His sharply pleated trousers were gracefully tailored down to his English shoes.

"I'm afraid there's not a lot to show you," he said.

In the dim, there wasn't much to see. With the exception of a cot in the corner, and brick and board bookcases lining the walls, only a small writing table at the window occupied the floor. If not for an elaborate, multicolored chart above a stack of *Wall Street Journals*, the four bare walls could have led one to believe they defined the cell of a monk.

It was then that I glimpsed the unmistakable white plastic radio on the desk—virtually feeling that dial in my fingers as though it were yesterday. Scanning stations like a Cold War operative in the never-ending darkness of my bedroom, I had searched for the *Beach Boys, Elvis, the Beatles*, if not for my own salvation. So, I remembered those hot summer nights of eternal adolescence, when the innocence of a boyhood lost gave way to the wisdom of love.

"I had a radio like that!" I enthused.

Pickett looked surprised.

"A twelfth birthday present! My uncle gave it to me when my aunt wasn't looking."

"I bought that in a pawn shop," Pickett confessed. "Over on the East Side!"

"When was that?" I asked him.

Pickett almost blushed. "Before I went to college."

Looking up at the multicolored chart, I continued my cross-examination. When I asked what it was, he started sidling in place, then slipped his hands into his pockets. He went over and picked up the newspaper he'd dropped, and put it on top of the pile.

"Do you read the *Wall Street Journal*?" I inquired.

"As a matter of fact, I do! In fact, I—play the market. Well—not exactly play it. I—theoretically play it!" He vaguely waved in the chart's direction. "And keep track of how I do over the year."

"It looks like you do pretty well!" I applauded, guessing he had trebled his holdings. "I wish I had your foresight!"

His self-effacing smile dismissed the compliment. "It's nothing, Brooke," Pickett replied. "It's really nothing at all."

"Tell me," I asked when we were underway, "how you decided to become a priest.

"I mean—" I attempted to excuse myself, "it's not—a usual choice these days."

For the first time, Pickett laughed—a self-deprecating laugh, as though the joke were on him. "I'm not sure!" he responded.

I wondered if he'd ever been asked the question.

"I guess…most of the careers I considered," he mused, "seemed like a waste of time."

"Did you always—believe in God?"

Pickett seemed intrigued by the question. "Not—as an idea," he pondered. "Only as a matter of the heart."

"And you met Athena at Columbia!" I raised another matter of the heart.

"Yes!" he said. "I roomed next-door to Ted."

"Did you know him well?"

"From what I could tell," he refused to take the bait, "there was no one better at tennis."

With the exception of several points of local interest, the trip to Newport was a silent one. But turning onto Ocean Drive, he sat up in his seat. Biting a fingernail, he appeared amazed by the manicured peninsula—as if taken by some unforeseen opportunity that may have lain at its end.

"This could be the easiest interview you've ever had," I said.

"The truth is," he said, "I don't like interviews."

"Think of it as dinner," I suggested.

"Thank you, Brooke," Pickett replied. "But I've never really liked dinner."

It is at least ironic that it would be at Ted's house, and under these circumstances, that I was brought back to that fleeting time in life when anything was possible. Pickett was the source of it—this unexplained, enigmatic priest—for having permeated the whole outdoors with the spirit of bygone youth. It was a spirit of hope, and of destiny, into which every child is born, and which gradually turns to unspoken despair in a world that has ceased to care.

He reminded me of every sweet summer evening that ever blessed me as a child, when the autocratic world of adulthood fell prey to weak-kneed romances and adolescent dreams. The redolent earthen spices of June wandered wildly across the broad lawn, now wet and blue beneath staccato sprinklers spitting rainbows into the sky. When we arrived at the front door, Pickett was blotting his face with a handkerchief—then quickly slipped it back into his pocket when he heard someone approaching.

We were shown past Ted's study to the back of the house. Pickett entered the sunroom before me, abruptly stopping at my nose. I knew without looking that he must have been standing face-to-face with Athena.

As her laughing eyes sparkled in the evening light, and her smile filled the fragrant room, I wondered if, despite the genetic odds, Athena would ever grow old. For in that moment, on that aromatic night, she was standing in the garden again. It was as though every goodness of her lost past had come back to haunt me with the beauty of that time—as though she wasn't tainted by the intervening years, nor paid the price the rest of us had paid.

"You're not a priest anymore!" she exclaimed.

Pickett's face was flushed. He reached into his pocket for the handkerchief and withdrew an empty hand.

"Where is your collar?" Athena inquired, shyly peering at him.

"I thought—I'd be a man tonight!"

Athena grinned. "That's still possible?"

As if on the brink of desperation, he came back, "I can only hope!"

"Ted is in the dining room with Leonard. Do you think you could join them, Father Pickett?"

Pickett hesitated, looked at me, then went ahead through the doorway.

Athena took my arm. "I wanted you to know there's no need to ask Pickett anything."

"I beg your pardon?"

"Ted says he doesn't care. And Leonard does whatever Ted does."

"It's already decided?"

"Of course not!" she laughed. "Pickett hasn't said, 'Yes'!"

As we entered the dining room, Pickett was standing alone in front of the hearth, while Ted and Leonard were intently conversing as they looked onto the courts below. Athena squeezed my arm, peering up at me with unexpectedly beseeching eyes. Whether she was pleading with me to keep the peace, or telling me she couldn't bear to stay, as she parted for the door, I knew it was mine to fend off Ted's attacks on Pickett.

When Ted caught sight of me, he called out my name and exuberantly waved me over. Turning to Pickett, I ushered him in, introducing my outcast friend.

"We've already met, Brooke!" Ted announced. "Pickett here went to Columbia with me! Before he became a holy man!"

Ted was drunk.

"Do you mean a priest?" I retaliated.

"Christ, you don't look like a priest. You're better looking than I remember—but you don't look like a priest. Leonard, does Pickett look like a priest? Christ, we need a priest for our church!"

Leonard, a thin middle-aged sort with a clipped mustache, vaguely nodded. He wore a green plaid suit in the heat, standing there as one who failed every social test except the gift of making money. Thus, he was a regular fixture on the Newport cocktail circuit, and until his recent resignation, the Treasurer of Trinity Church.

With Athena gone, I took up the challenge of curbing Ted in his inebriated state. Despite my attempts to redirect the conversation, Ted's single-mindedness was clearly fixed on making Pickett his prey.

"Ted, who takes care of the courts?" I asked.

"I do," he warded me off. "So, what would make a man become a priest?" he laughed. "It sure as hell isn't the money!

"Is it the collar?" Ted winked at me. "What a way to get a woman!"

Pickett reached for his handkerchief, then let his brow perspire.

"I mean, what kind of woman would marry a priest?"

"Or a tennis player." Athena had slipped back into the room—if not in the nick of time.

"The kind who wants to be rich and famous!"

"Or wanted to be rich and famous."

"Who doesn't want to be rich and famous?"

Athena tilted her head. "Then I must have married the wrong man," she teased.

"Who's over the hill?" Ted demanded.

"In a town like Newport, who isn't?" she said.

"Speak for yourself!" Ted retorted.

Athena's lovely eyes fixed on him. "I'm speaking for us all," she calmly replied. "I'm speaking for our whole generation."

"Pickett here is part of our generation. And by the way—not rich or famous!"

"Maybe he doesn't want to be," she said, turning to her dinner guest. "Do you want to be rich and famous, Father Pickett?"

"I guess—I never thought it really mattered."

"Lucky for you!" Ted guffawed. "You'll never be disappointed!"

The dining room was a capacious space of timber and old-world varnish. The evening sun washed the air in tawny light, a warm breeze blew through the terrace doors, making the sheer white curtains dance, and out on the horizon a sailboat rhythmically rocked on the water. The silence of summer filled the room, save the distant collisions of serving silver and a faint popping sound of a tennis match somewhere down on the lawn.

As we sat down, I suddenly realized that none of this seemed right. It wasn't just the interview that seemed like a charade. The whole thing seemed like a charade—the room, the house, the life we were living in this strangely unanchored time.

It was the world of our parents and grandparents, who had raised this town from the sea, and a land that imposed no limits on them for as far as the eye could see. Though the Adams built scores of houses like this in two hundred American years, for the first time I sensed our time had run out, and we had been left to pretend.

Unlike our forebears, we'd come to believe that we stood on the brink of the end, where our only recourse was forsaking the past for the sake of exploiting the present. Ours was the way of deriding yesterday by the boastful claims of our time, and forgetting the heart, and striving, and hope, that had made its monuments great. Humility came at too great cost in the face of our mortgaged future, and so we were left with only ourselves to revere and to celebrate.

This was what Athena saw in him, I thought as he whispered grace: a man who believed in heroes and hope, in God and in destiny. Pickett believed in a past we did not, however we wanted to, drawing him back to his childhood hopes, back to his firstborn dreams. If we came to believe in only ourselves as the authors of our salvation—trading the wisdom of yesterday for the illusions of tomorrow—in the process, we had sentenced ourselves to the prison of the present, where we were left to live and to die by the icons of the moment.

Enthroning himself at the head of the table, Ted started in, "Do you play tennis?"

"No, I don't," Pickett replied.

"Do you play golf?" he asked.

"I'm afraid not."

"Do you ride?"

"Horses?" Pickett inquired.

Ted burst into laughter.

"Yes, horses," I said.

"Very little," Pickett said.

"But more than tennis or golf," Ted said.

"Yes, more than tennis or golf."

Pickett's easy deflection of the cross-examination clearly aggravated Ted, who, like a dog with a bone, wagged his head and said, "Now—I don't get it. The last time I knew, you were going back to wherever the hell you came from."

Pickett nodded.

"To work for your old man."

Pickett remained composed.

"In the newspaper business, wasn't it?" Ted said. He shared a glare around the table. "But then I never understood how a newspaper heir could be on scholarship—can you, Leonard?"

Leonard pursed his lips.

"Then all of a sudden, you're in the same town as Elizabeth!" Ted barked into his drink. "What a coincidence! Isn't that a coincidence, Leonard?"

Ted stared for a long moment at his captive hostage—one of those penetrating, drunken stares one fears is onto something. "Though I don't remember you ever went to church," he clenched the bone again.

"How would we know?" Athena intervened. "We were never around."

"Around enough to know we haven't heard the whole story—that there's another story to be told."

Columbia had always been a strange place of brilliant eccentrics and New York socialites. Clearly failing the former, Ted spent his days at the New York Athletic Club, and his nights downtown, wherever the latest restaurant happened to be. And for reasons I had yet to understand, Athena faithfully followed.

"Now, I want to get something straight," Ted said, turning his fork on Pickett. "This town isn't what you're used to up there in the hills of Massachusetts. We don't have crazies like Elizabeth living here in Newport."

"And if Ted has his way," Athena interceded, "it's going to stay that way."

"Athena wants Elizabeth to live with us!" Ted defended himself. "Christ, everyone knows Elizabeth's elevator doesn't run to the top!"

"She's not as deficient as some people I know in Newport," Athena rejoined.

"Athena's talking about me," Ted imparted, peering blearily around the table. "I was the dumb one at Columbia. I might have been the best tennis player in the country, but I was the dumb one in school."

"Which is why I could never leave you," she quipped. "You've made far too much money."

It was as if Pickett missed the irony, which left the rest of us amused.

"And I," Ted roared, "could never leave Athena! I'm afraid Elizabeth would shoot me!"

"Elizabeth would never do that," Athena smirked. "She only shoots unfaithful men."

"And what about unfaithful women?"

"She doesn't know any," Athena said.

By dinner's end, the conversation had parted ways—Pickett, on a path to Athena's childhood, and Ted, loudly pontificating on the ethics of successful business. The sounds of tennis were gone from the lawn, offering momentary peace, and the steady staccato of spitting sprinklers was finally put to rest. Left to gaze at the stranded sloop, outlined in running lights, I considered my own uncertain future, as it certainly waited for sleep.

"So, Leonard!" Ted started in again, through an audible sip of brandy. "What do you have for me?"

Stopping in mid-sentence, Pickett wisely yielded the table to our host.

"Have I got a stock for you!" Leonard said, pouncing on the opportunity. "It's at one-ten a share, but I'm telling you, Ted, in six months it's going ten times—maybe twenty!"

Ted looked skeptically at Leonard.

"It's a sure thing!" Leonard cried. "They're about to hit!"

"Hit what?"

"Gold!" Leonard wheezed.

"Gold," Ted sarcastically came back.

"They're already mining on seven sites!"

Ted barely raised a brow. "Where?"

"In the Amazon! With ten million acres of mineral rights, they could go on forever!"

Ted looked at me across the table, as though the two of us knew better. "What are they mining, fool's gold?" he said, pleased with his abortive jeu de mots.

"Ted, you know I'm a hedge fund man. But this is the exception! The garimpeiros are panning the streams like nothing they've ever seen!"

"Who the hell are the garimpeiros?"

"The prospectors—in Brazil!"

"So?" Ted leered.

"So, there has to be a hard-rock source not far behind!"

"And why isn't this wonder stock at twenty a share?"

"They haven't found the source! But when they do—twenty, in a bull gold market, maybe forty dollars a share!"

Ted got up and went to the sideboard. "No thanks, Leonard. This is one of your fly-by-nighters I'll have to pass up."

"How many times have I steered you wrong?" Leonard dejectedly replied.

"Leonard, what am I worth?" Ted barked, returning with another brandy. "Ten million?"

"Nine—give or take a couple hundred thousand."

"A guy's worth ten—maybe eleven million dollars. Why would he gamble it away?"

"To make ten million more," Leonard said.

Ted bore down on Pickett. "And what would I do with ten million more? Christ, I can't spend my dividends as it is!"

"Don't say I didn't warn you," Leonard shrugged.

"I mean, why would I need junk stock? We're in the longest bull in history! The Dow's topped twenty-four hundred!"

"You never know what interest rates are going to do."

"Interest rates, hell!" Ted scoffed. "When they go up, I make it in futures. When they go down, I make it in bonds.

You know as well as I do, Leonard—I've never been able to lose!"

"It's how big you win," Leonard counseled.

"I'm a blue-chip man. When you've made the kind of money I've made," Ted crowed, "you become a blue-chip man." He turned to me. "Brooke, you must be a blue-chip man."

"What's a blue-chip man?"

Ted ignored the snub. "I'm making it on mergers anyway," he said.

"And insider trading?" I goaded.

"Insider trading, my ass," he grumbled. "That's all you ever hear about—insider trading! Anyway, what's wrong with insider trading? As long as it lines the pockets!"

"What's the name of the stock?" Pickett unexpectedly spoke up.

"Treasure Valley," Leonard said.

"Treasure Valley!" Ted mocked.

A tray of champagne flutes appeared from the pantry and was set in front of Ted. "What does it matter to you, Father Pickett? You planning to invest your parson's salary in mining stocks?" he laughed.

I almost mentioned Pickett's talent in the market, but thankfully thought better of it.

"Athena, you *did* tell him," Ted said, picking up the bottle.

Oddly flustered, Athena hesitated. "I didn't have a chance."

"We're toasting the new rector, and he doesn't know what he's getting? It's twenty-two thousand and the apartment in town. That's our final offer."

Pickett didn't respond. He was either one hell of a poker player, or he didn't give a damn.

"It must be twice what you're getting up there in Massachusetts!"

"There's no—rectory?" Pickett hesitated, barely shy of a lament.

"There was!" Ted happily shared the news. "It was a helluva house! As big as mine! But we couldn't keep it up. Now we have the little place above the drugstore—right across the street from Brooke!"

Pickett seemed disheartened.

"More than enough for a bachelor like you!"

"Is that it?" Athena defiantly came back. "Or is it that we like to keep our clergy poor so we don't have to be?"

"Christ, Athena, the last one we had was better endowed than the church!"

Turning to me, Athena's face was crimson. "Brooke, what do you think?"

"About what?" I ducked.

"About whether or not clergy are underpaid."

"I'm not sure—" I heroically hedged, "how to put a price on a vocation."

"Exactly my point!" Ted triumphantly pronounced. "Ministers shouldn't get paid!"

Athena sympathetically peered at Pickett before frustration got the better of her. "You see, John," she said, with that sparkling directness which made her so enchanting, "if our clergy weren't poor, they would be of no use. The only way the rich can be rid of their guilt is to be blessed by someone who isn't."

She gazed at Pickett, like an erstwhile lover who didn't want to say goodbye. "To be an angel to the rich, you have to be poor. Otherwise, we shoot the messenger."

Ted got up and disappeared outside with a magnum of champagne in his fist. As odd-man-out, Leonard followed his client onto the terrace. Perhaps seizing the chance, Pickett looked across the table at Athena; and like a fitful adolescent, anxiously asked, "Do you wish I had a bigger house?"

Athena looked back with utter admiration. "I wish you had the biggest house in Newport."

A loud pop sounded like a toy gun on the terrace—and then a triumphant, "Whoop!"

"Well," Ted sighed, coming back in, "do we have a deal?" As he filled the flutes on the serving tray, Leonard played the dutiful server; and when Ted raised his glass, Pickett raised his own in ceremonial agreement.

"Good," Ted said, taking down the contents in a gulp. "I'm going to bed!"

I didn't know if arrangements had been made for Pickett's overnight accommodation, so at one, I offered him a room in my house and a ride home the next day. Pickett looked relieved, though deferring to Athena to be sure it met with her approval. And by two, she was leaning against the front door, bidding us goodbye.

As I watched her in the moonlight, her head barely canted and peering at my dazed companion, for the first time I glimpsed the impossible beauty she must have engendered in him. Looking back at Pickett, I wondered if anything had changed in him since his youth, and why I sensed that in spite of the unrest, nothing really had. Pickett was as much an heir to Liverpool—to Marilyn, the Kennedys, the twist—yet I couldn't imagine him past 1965, when the country began to fall apart.

If Pickett saw it coming in a way we never did, and retreated to a time of God and love, as we left the house, I almost believed his world could come together again. It was as if the rest of us had agreed to a pact that the past was irrelevant, and forged ahead on the ignorant assumption that we were smarter than our fathers. As naïve as Pickett appeared to me on that strange, romantic night, little did I know that when all was said and done, we were the most naïve of all.

Since Pickett had come unprepared, I managed to rustle up a pair of pajamas and a threadbare smoking jacket. As we sat together in my upstairs study, there was something paradoxically fitting about his having donned that paisley garment as surrogate lord of the manor. Fitting in the sense that the garment didn't fit, as regal as he may have appeared—that the restlessness agitating his frame denied sartorial confinement.

In retrospect, Pickett never looked quite right in any of the finery he wore, from the first tailored suit I underhandedly financed to the several that would follow. They never seemed to fit, however faithfully they clung to his willowy frame—as though his energy defied the limits of his ectomorphic profile. If at first, I ascribed his incongruous manner to social awkwardness, there was something in his guileless way that transcended social convention.

More than once, Pickett went over to the window that looked onto his future dwelling. "At first, it might *seem* small," he would remark, bearing down on the apartment, "but after you look at it a while, it does appear rather large." Then he would return to the center of the room to further consider the matter—as though, if he thought about it long enough, it was sure to expand before his eyes.

Day was dawning as he continued to peer out the window with his back to me. I was about to propose that we get some sleep when he suddenly turned around. Out of left field, Pickett asked, "What does the church do for the poor?"

"The—church?" I repeated.

"Yes," he replied.

"I'm not—exactly sure. I know it gives away a lot of money."

"Are there slums in Newport?"

"Yes," I said. "'West of Broadway'."

"Is it far from here?"

"Several miles. Or depending on your yardstick, several thousand miles."

He nodded again.

"Is that a problem?"

"No, Brooke, it's not a problem."

"What—is it?" I addressed his look of puzzlement.

"It just isn't the church," he said.

"Do you think—you're making a mistake?" I asked.

"A mistake?" Pickett inquired.

"In coming to Newport."

"Oh, no, Brooke!" he said. "There's really no such thing."

"No such thing?" I skeptically responded.

"Not as long as there's tomorrow."

Suggesting that 'tomorrow' was fast approaching, I told him I was going to bed. Taking my announcement as a condemnation of his 'own long-winded diatribe', he apologized for what he penitently deemed an 'inexcusable insensitivity'. When I succeeded in convincing him otherwise, he appeared to be relieved—then asked if I would 'terribly' mind his staying up a while longer.

Several hours later, I groggily woke up and made a pot of coffee. Stealing up the stairs to see if Pickett was awake, before I could look down the hall, I saw him sitting in the slip-covered chair, peering out the window. Like the night before, he brought back to me every blind aspiration of my youth—every naïve striving for the unseen future which is the stuff of growing up—but which begins to dissipate into that cynical age which no longer believes in itself, vanishing into the world of work only months after college.

When he saw me, he jumped up, closed my smoking jacket, and bade me a bright good morning. A ball-point pen was tucked behind an ear. The spiral notebook he was holding in his hand was covered with a tapestry of numbers—multiplied, divided, added and subtracted in as many directions.

"Would you like some breakfast?"

"No, Brooke, thanks. I'm really not very hungry. I suspect when you undergo life changes like this, you're never really hungry."

I tried to remember if I had lost weight moving back to Newport.

"Say, Brooke, do you happen to know a town near Providence, called 'Six Bridges'?"

When I told him that I did, he asked if I could take him on the way back to Massachusetts. He explained he had family business to take care of, and that it wouldn't take more than an hour. As it was on the way, and the summer day was mine, I happily obliged—giving rise to a litany of thanks, and a request to use the telephone.

Respecting his privacy, I retreated down the stairs and poured a second cup of coffee. When he appeared in the kitchen, he looked ebullient, as if the last piece of a challenging puzzle had finally found its place. His restless uncertainty, the anxious fits and starts that dogged him through dinner at the Talbots, were spectacularly gone— unaccountably redeemed by a countenance of conviction.

"I just realized," I apologized, "you haven't even seen the church!"

"No, I haven't. I hear it's a lovely landmark building," he replied.

"Would you like to see it?"

"Oh, no, Brooke, thanks. I'll see it when I arrive."

When we were underway, I curiously asked, "Why do you want the job?"

"I'm not sure," he pondered. "I guess it feels…it feels like it was meant to be."

"Like it was destined?" I asked.

"That's it!" he said. "It feels like it was destined." I remember him peering intently through the windshield. "It may not have always seemed—destined," he mused. "But I realize now that it was."

As I silently considered this last exchange, Pickett seemed eerily at peace. It was as though we had lighted on the final definition of all for which he had longed—even on the word, which may have eluded him as much as the destiny itself. Yet, happy as I was to have given voice to another man's fanciful vision, a palpable fear welled in my gut that somehow it wouldn't be enough.

"Brooke," he finally broke the silence. "Do you believe in destiny?"

"I'm not sure," I admitted.

"Did you ever?" he asked.

I hesitated. "Yes," I said.

"What happened?" he pursued me.

"I'm not sure," I confessed. "I really… can't remember."

Six Bridges got its name by the peculiar fact that the only way in and out of town was across a run of six railroad bridges. After the War, the bridges were closed and converted to automobile traffic, and ever since, the freight yard had lain beneath a windblown veil of grass and weeds, abandoned. The last remnants of the industrious life that once had raged there were two lone boxcars, parked like empty tombs next to a boarded-up station.

I knew something about Six Bridges, and several other mill towns on the way to New Haven. As a child, the mill towns lingered in my mind as a time better left forgotten, but living on a campus of pristine brick and ivy, I was starved for unadulterated texture. On many hot summer nights during nepotistic summer internships at the family bank, I found myself exploring their libraries, digging up the sins of the past.

On the edge of his seat, Pickett took charge of navigating the route, instructing me to turn onto Elmwood Avenue and proceed to the end of the street. It was a section of Six Bridges that I had never seen. Unfamiliar as I was with the neighborhood, which had obviously sprouted in the fifties, there was something about its ubiquitous spirit that made me feel like I had been there before.

Tiny box-top houses laid out row upon row on an unyielding flat of land, gave me to infer block upon block for as far as the eye could see. I didn't need Yale's art survey course to come to the aesthetic conclusion that the infamous 'raised ranch' was a low-water mark in American architecture. Yet, painstakingly kept on postage stamp lots across a spectrum of peeling pastels, I felt at once the pathos of their working-class hope, and the fear it was about to be lost.

For all the pinks and greens and robin's-egg blues, I could have guessed Pickett's would be white. Impeccably painted, with forest green shutters, it enjoyed an oversized front yard. If there were a way the pedestrian 'cape' could emit a classical presence, then its proprietor, of surely modest means, was as certainly up to the task.

A short round man in a mustard-yellow jacket was hard at work on the lawn, intently pounding a sign into the ground, 'Dapper Real Estate'. Before we could get out, he rushed the car and offered his hand through Pickett's window. Having to wait until the hand was withdrawn to exit the passenger door, Pickett seemed pleasantly taken aback by the agent's enthusiasm.

He wore a golf-themed hat that protected his head from the ravages of the sun—whose synthetic thatch of green and dissected plastic ball gave the illusion of 'buried in the rough'. His small-town smile would have been ideal for an advertising circular. As Pickett was about to make the introduction, Mr. Dapper handed me his card. "I'm a self-made man," he happily declared, "and I think I did a damn good job!"

"Brooke, would you excuse us?" Pickett intervened in an abruptly businesslike manner. "I need to discuss several things with Mr. Dapper, then we can be on our way."

As they disappeared through the diminutive front door, I decided to go for a walk. Despite that Pickett's past remained obscure, it made sense that it had started here. However claustrophobic it may have been for a boundless soul like John Pickett, it was a world with a center, a rhythm, a sense, in an increasingly nonsensical time.

Before I left the yard, an elderly gentleman waved from the far side of the street. Descending from his stoop, he charged ahead. "Was that Jackie Pickett?" he quizzically asked, offering his hand across the fence.

"John Pickett—yes," I equivocated. "Though I suspect, one and the same!"

The silver-thin mustache on his upper lip made him look like he hailed from the forties. "Good God," he replied, "I haven't seen that son of a gun in ten years!"

He had a genial, engaging, block-like face, and ruddy Irish complexion. I introduced myself. "Nice to meet ya', Brooke. The name's JD O'Neill!

"From across the street, yeah," he went on. "The wife and I are retired ova' there."

"So, you knew him as a boy!" I launched my surreptitious investigation.

He pridefully nodded, then glanced at Pickett's house. "Been empty since he went to college."

"Did you know his family?"

"When they was around—sure! Heck of a nice people! 'Course, the fatha' had a bit of a problem with the bottle. That's what did him in. And the wife, she up and remarried in a month. So, Jackie was left with Uncle Gordie."

"Gordon?" I inquired.

"Gordie, the clown! Yeah—used to be in the circus. Never was all there. When Jackie's old man died, he got sent back behind the green fence.

"The mental institution, yeah," he clarified, addressing my look of confusion. He peered up at the sky and burst into laughter. "The wife always said they was a case for evolution! From Gordie and the brotha', to little Jackie Pickett!" He shook his Irish head. "Who would 'a thought a little prince like Jackie could come from a family like that? Can you imagine? Lived alone three years before he went off to college!"

"How did he—survive?" I shamelessly pried.

"Three papah routes!" He shook his head. "Has he made his first million?"

"He's a priest," I said.

"A priest?" he winced, looking stunned.

"An Episcopal priest."

"An Episcopal priest! Don't see many of them in these parts!"

"Though not a typical Episcopal priest."

"I guess I shouldn't be surprised. Every summer," he recalled, "Jackie had a camp for kids he'd bring up from the projects.

"I always wondered," he puzzled, with a sparkle in his eye, "if he saw himself in them waifs and strays!"

"Where were the paper routes?"

"Two was in Six Bridges. The other was in Providence, yeah.

"Ova' on the East Side! The only reason I know is, I took him there in a blizza'd. I somehow had a sense he dreamed of living there one day." He laughed. "And I believed he would!

"But damn, he was a helluva businessman! I'll never forget the deal he cut with his silk stockin' customah's. He'd charge a penny for takin' their old newspapahs back— and then he'd go down to fisherman's wharf and sell the papah's as fish wrap!

"Three ways to make a buck!" JD marveled. "I used to tell him he ran his own Trifecta! And what a whiz with numbers! He knew what he'd made before he even counted it!"

A car horn sounded from across the street. "Gotta go!" he said. "Nice to meet ya', Brooke! The wife needs a ride to the mall! And if I don't catch him," he called across the street, "give ole Jackie our regards!

"And I wouldn't write him off!" he cautioned from the yard. "He may make them millions yet!"

As I turned back to the house, Mr. Dapper was exiting the front door. "Nice little home!" he appraised it on the move. "John is just saying goodbye!" Then, winking with professional authority, he said, "A case of seller's remorse."

I went back to Six Bridges several times that summer. At first, I thought it was simply out of patronizing pity for the place. It was a world-lost town, and there were few things I found sadder—a town no one cared about, which could have disappeared from the face of the earth and never be noticed.

But by summer's end I realized my ritual returns were more than affected condescension. I wasn't sure what it was. There was something unsettlingly powerful about its desolation—something seductive about its spirit, which wandered there in the lonely streets, drifted through the shattered glass of ghostly mills, and dwelt in the silence of those dog day afternoons.

For out of the haunts of this broken dream rose a memory of every human aspiration which had ever driven this land; every fancy, naïveté and impossible hope that ever rattled in the basements of Edison, Ford, and the million men who never made it—every romance, belief, and unreachable vision of a life of love and longing. Out of the flickering neon, out of the grand deserted hotels on Main Street, out of the great boarded theater named Victory, thirty years now hollow as a drum, came the truth that there was once a life of conviction, where nothing was impossible, save the deathly decision that it might be so.

And in that moment, I believed that such was the seed of this once flourishing land. It was not the merchant traders, not the robber barons—it was not the new young entrepreneurs who had long since taken credit. It was the spirit of those who had dreamed in the rubble, with an unquenchable thirst for tomorrow.

Chapter 5

I'd be a liar to deny that I looked across the street without fail every August night, in hopes of detecting some sign of life in the windows above the drugstore. Though I knew the odds were increasingly great that the light would finally appear, unfilled expectations have a way of threatening eternity. When it finally came, it was Labor Day—that mystifying mark when we celebrate work by assiduously not working—and committed to the task, I spent the day at odds with any kind of work, save fretting about how little I'd achieved in my outwardly successful life.

Night had fallen, and the damp nocturnal air was settling in the street when I screwed up my courage and braved a walk beneath the illuminated windows. Captive of my own charade, I avoided looking up—nonchalantly crossing the empty street as though evening walks were a habit. Just as I was passing the great weeping beech in the middle of Pickett's front yard, I discerned a shadowy figure tracing the sinuous lines of the tree.

"Hello, Brooke!" I heard out of the dark.

I started—before catching my breath.

"Sorry!" Pickett said, coming out to the walk. "I didn't mean to scare you!"

"Not at all!" I swallowed my heart. "I was just—out for a stroll!"

He was dressed in the same pressed linen suit he had worn to dinner at the Talbots. For the first time in my life, I felt underdressed while out for a spontaneous saunter.

"Brooke, I wanted to thank you," he said.

I remember feeling perplexed.

"For our talk on the way to Six Bridges!" he said.

Drawing a blank, I nodded.

"The truth is," he said, "I had never thought about it. But you were right—I believe in destiny!"

Unexpectedly jealous, I replied, "You're lucky."

"It isn't luck," he said.

"What is it?" I asked.

He looked confused—as though I had lost the train of thought.

"If it isn't luck, what is it?" I repeated.

He laughed, "Brooke, it's destiny!"

I didn't see Pickett for several days when I stopped in early at the drugstore, where he was sitting at the end of the soda fountain, sipping a cup of coffee. Wearing his immaculate linen suit, he had donned a clerical collar. I was hesitant to intrude on what appeared to be a solitary moment, but as the register rang out my tube of toothpaste, Pickett instinctively looked up.

"Brooke!" he called, jumping up from his stool. He pointed to the seat next to his. I thanked him for the offer to buy me breakfast, but agreed to a cup of coffee—grateful as I was to have a friend in this increasingly alien town.

"I'm sorry I haven't been over," he said. "Getting my bearings, and so on."

I told him not to worry.

"By the way," he said, "you mentioned 'West of Broadway'."

I remembered that I had.

"It looks like there's work to be done down there."

I guiltily agreed. The truth was, the church's legacy and wealth that began with the robber barons had cast a long shadow down the Avenue to that all-but-forgotten side of town. And as one who resided cheek-to-jowl with their well-heeled, if fading descendants, I had averted my eyes from those hard-luck skids no less than the rest of them.

"I was thinking about a newspaper project the church could undertake."

It was hard to imagine any member of the church who would even know how to get there.

"You might want to run it by the vestry," I advised, not wanting to sound pessimistic.

"Good idea," Pickett said.

"From what I can tell, they like to be informed."

"I was going to ask," he said, switching gears, "if you've seen the Talbots lately."

I told him I hadn't, but that if they weren't at home, they were probably in New York.

"A special trip?" he inquired.

"They usually go once or twice a month," I said.

"Do you have an idea—when they might be back?"

I regretted that I didn't.

"I thought I should probably call on them," he said. "I mean, given their role in the search."

I granted him the point.

"And as gracious as they were to host the dinner party."

As 'gracious' wasn't the adjective that immediately came to mind, I defaulted to my cup in hopes of moving on to another subject.

"They have a beautiful house," he said, looking brighter.

"They do," I had to agree.

"It could be the biggest in Newport," he said. "With the exception of the mansions, of course."

"Though few of them are still lived in," I offered.

"Why is that?" he queried.

"That kind of living is a thing of the past."

"Five million for Rosecliff," he noted. I was curious to know how he had gleaned what was somewhat rarefied knowledge.

"It's been on the market for years," I said. "The Preservation Society wants to buy it."

"That would be a shame," he surprisingly replied. "That would be a real shame."

Pickett seemed to do well for his first Sunday in what his predecessor described as "an intimidating church in an intimidating town." Despite the prospect of his oratory prowess, I was relieved that he continued to forgo the sermon at the 8 o'clock service. If brevity was the soul of wit, for me it was a glimpse of salvation.

Yet, watching him preside at the liturgy that morning, the remarkable paradox I observed at Elizabeth's wedding reappeared. Then I had viewed it as a contradiction—some conflict that must have raged within him—but in our meetings since, I came to perceive it as an ingenious balance: an incorporation of all that was possible in his waking world of promise, with all that was not. So, the fitful antics of his personality were given to the world as a tremoring oscillation between a state of utter nervousness, and one of utter grace.

Filing out of church toward the sunlit doorway, I watched him standing on the steps, greeting the aging congregation with all the charm it could have hoped for. Stripped of his vestments, I noticed that again he was wearing his linen suit—impressively free of the predictable wrinkles in the sweltering heat. Though I have always been anything but impulsive, as part of the sartorial crowd, I felt oddly responsible for Pickett's limited wardrobe.

Stepping into an empty pew, I waited for the end of the line, and was able to greet him without the distraction of lurking parishioners. "Are you doing anything at noon?" I asked.

"Brooke, I don't believe I am!"

"Would you like to come by for a drink?" I proposed.

"Well—yes," he hesitated.

Sensing he might have another engagement, I replied, "Only if it works!"

"Oh, no! Just an—uncertainty!" he said. "That would be terrific!"

"See you at noon!" I said, from the walk.

"At noon!" Pickett repeated.

"Say, Brooke," he called, as I stepped off the curb, "you haven't seen the Talbots lately!"

"No," I called back, "I'm afraid I haven't!"

He waved. "See you at noon!"

Pickett was standing on my front step at high noon, holding a small leather suitcase. Exchanging pleasantries, he dropped it in the hall and came into the living room. He was an appreciative audience, surveying the space with liberal admiration.

Scanning the books lining the walls, his eyes fixed on a secretary that came from the manse in Providence, and was the best piece in the house. A light was on above my typewriter, drawing him to the corner. An expansive blueprint of a Concordia yawl lay unrolled on the desk.

"Is that a Concordia?" Pickett inquired.

"It is!" I said, intrigued.

"It's a beautiful boat," he thoroughly approved.

"The most brilliant wooden boat ever made."

"What do they run these days?" he asked.

I wasn't sure what he was asking.

"What would a Concordia 39 cost?"

"Oh—it depends on the condition. I would think you could get a really good one for about fifty thousand."

"Wow," he replied, "that's a lot of money!"

"Less than Rosecliff!" I cracked.

Pickett laughed. "But more than I've got! Fifty thousand more than I've got!"

I offered him a gin and tonic, which he gratefully accepted; and with drinks in hand, we made our way through the summer kitchen to the garden. As we sat down, I asked how he thought his first Sunday in Newport had gone. Apparently preoccupied, he said that he thought it went well.

"Have you gotten to know many parishioners?" I asked.

"Some," he vaguely responded.

"Of course, you know the Talbots. But I was wondering if you'd like to get to know some of the others."

"I'm sure I will in time," he distractedly rejoined. "But thanks, Brooke—for the thought."

"Mrs. Chatham would like to host a reception."

"Thank her for me, will you, Brooke?"

"She lives on Bellevue Avenue."

Pickett looked up. "In one of the mansions?" he asked.

"No," I confessed. "But it's a lovely modern house, looking out over the Sound."

"That's very kind…" his voice trailed off.

I laughed. "So, the answer is no?"

"I don't mean to be ungrateful," he said, "but it's not the sort of thing I like to do."

When I saw him begin to look at his watch, I decided to get on with it. Drawing out an envelope from inside my blazer, I handed it to him. As he opened it, I noticed that one of his pant legs was fastidiously stitched across what I imagined must have been a significant tear in the fabric.

It was a gift of a thousand dollars, I explained, "from an anonymous parishioner," which I proceeded to lie had been privately laundered through my personal checkbook. In accordance with the donor's wishes, the money could be used for his wardrobe, "or anything else you might need," I fibbed, "in a town like Newport."

Fearful that he had seen through the ruse to the truth that I was the donor, it appeared that any like suspicion hadn't occurred to him. In fact, rather than appearing compromised by his unnamed patron, he seemed unduly grateful, ending with the query, "I don't suppose you could tell me who—"

"I'm afraid it's confidential," I said.

He nodded agreeably.

"An—interested party," I fumbled the ball.

Pickett knowingly smiled.

Worried he had come to the wrong conclusion, I suggested that we have some lunch.

"Oh, no, Brooke, thanks. At the 10 o'clock service, Athena asked me over for a swim."

Glad that Pickett wouldn't be alone on his first Sunday in Newport, despite lingering qualms, I was grateful that she had risen to the occasion.

"Though you were right," he said, picking up his suitcase. "They *were* in New York—Ted still is!"

"You'll be well taken care of," I assured my friend.

"It would have been good to see him."

In September's early days, as autumn fills the air with all that summer's lease would not allow, I saw little more of Pickett. Whether it was his schedule or mine, I wasn't sure, as I often found myself gone from the house, running here and there against fall's fate of wishing life's plans were not always too late. I had finished the story on the Concordia, and had little to work on then—save the not irrelevant question of what to do with the rest of my life.

Ted's liking of 'a good listener', as he put it, began to show itself at this time, and he was soon calling several times a week to invite me to the Hall for lunch. At first, I didn't understand it, as different as we were, but after several engagements I realized that for some unknown reason, he trusted me. Unlike his coterie of admirers, who loitered about in search of something he might give them— a glance, a smile, a shredded piece of salvation from a discarded tennis ball—he knew I had little interest in tennis, and even less in that order of devotion.

And in a guarded way, Ted intrigued me. He rarely made efforts in anyone's direction, let alone took pains to dine in the gallery overlooking Centre Court. But I discovered the sage way to enjoy a man like Ted was the way of caution; and despite regular contact, I managed to retain a careful distance.

"Brooke, you're a strange son of a bitch," he said, one afternoon.

"What does that mean?"

"The contradictions—Christ, you're full of them."

"The contradictions…" I responded.

"Don't play dumb with me." He looked out over Centre Court. "The word is, when your great-grandfather was born, he was the richest baby in the world."

"And look where it got him."

"Where?" he took the bait.

"My great-grandfather's dead," I said.

"That's what I mean!" he impatiently came back. "You try to deny your past!"

"I'm proud of my past," I held him at bay. "It's the future I'm worried about."

If his gaze wasn't vacant, it was at best blank.

"This doesn't bother you?" I asked.

"What doesn't bother me?"

"This!" I cast a glance at Centre Court.

He shrugged his powerful shoulders. "There are winners and losers," he matter-of-factly said. "We just happen to be the winners."

"And what about the losers?"

He smugly grinned. "You just said it—they're losers."

"So, that's where we've come?"

"It's where we've always been! Survival of the fittest!"

"So—*we're* the winners?" I theatrically marveled.

"It's why we're here, having lunch!"

"Then why do I feel like a loser?" I said.

"What would make you feel like a winner?"

Bearing down on him until I had his attention, I dryly replied, "Athena."

He scowled, peered back, then finally laughed. "You son of a bitch," he said.

When I surrendered a smile, he looked relieved. "She's beautiful. I'll give her that."

"She's more than beautiful," I said.

"Thank God you're just a friend."

"Christ, Ted, Athena is your wife!"

His beady eyes fixed on me. "You know as well as I do," he said, "marriage doesn't matter anymore."

Ted had a mind one would never call intelligent, and always recognize as clever. It was a mind that had allowed him to become a champion: ruthlessly strategic, cunningly subtle, and all churning beneath the ignorant assumption that no one else deserved to win. It was his capacity to manipulate—a tennis racket, an opponent, and anything else that lurked about the ragged ends of his universe— which marked Ted Talbot as an enviable study in the need to be victorious.

Everyone knew Ted's instinct to win was born from the loins of his father. Chip Talbot was one of those affluent fathers who'd devoted his adulthood to creating a life he lacked the foresight to live the first time around. So he would be seen in the celebrity box at every major tournament, bearing down from under a conspicuous hat as though the future of his fragile world depended on the victory of his son.

This may have been the source of my tolerance for Ted—knowing how fated his future had been, and that the misfortune of his injured knee came about by no fault of his own. It may also have come from sympathy for his having hailed from Great Neck, and the plight of such an insurance man with an enormous salary and almost no wealth. Still, if it is true that you are where you come from, Marblehead would have been a more fitting birthplace for a man like Ted 'Tizzy' Talbot.

When the two of us met for the last time of the season, Ted was wearing a navy-blue blazer and shimmering white pants. As I climbed the stairs to the gallery, he was standing in the midst of a pastel flock of middle-aged women competing for his autograph. Seeing me, he announced that he had to go, leaving fawning fans empty-handed.

"So, what do you think of our Father Pickett?" he asked as we were sitting down.

I told him I had grown to like him in the short time he had been in Newport.

"I didn't ask if you liked him!" Ted protested. "I said, what do you think of him as a priest?"

The truth is, I'd never thought of Pickett as a priest. It was not that I didn't trust his commitment; it was either that he was too great for the role, or the God the role presumed was too small. In either case, it was difficult to entertain this quixotic guardian of the faith—this unexplained, eccentric, clandestine romantic who hailed from a mysterious past—abiding so lifeless a social convention as the institutional church, in a time when the past to which it was bound appeared to have no future at all.

Ted shook his head. "I don't know," he said, answering his own question. "He has this half-assed idea about starting a newspaper to feed the goddam homeless." He laughed into his drink. "Thank God I convinced the Senior Warden to shoot that one down!"

"What do you have against him?" I asked.

"There's just something funny about Pickett. I mean, I knew him in college. I don't remember he was any great religious freak."

"What was he?" I pretended neutrality.

"I don't know," he growled. "From what I could tell, he was just another Poindexter with his nose in the books."

Rattling the ice in his double-martini, he peered onto the court below. "But that's not all," he finally confided. "I could tell he had a thing for women. Now that doesn't seem right."

"What doesn't seem right?"

"A priest with a thing for women!"

"Episcopal priests aren't celibate," I said.

"That isn't the goddam point! As far as I'm concerned, you give your life to God, you give your life to God—that's it!"

He tipped an ice cube into his mouth, and in a startling display, spat it over the railing, just missing a silver-haired player readying to serve. The gentleman looked up in a fit of outrage, then seeing it was Ted, showed a miraculous change of heart and offered a hearty wave.

"And then to end up in the same town as Elizabeth—Jesus Christ!" he balked. "He only works on Sundays as far as I can tell—and for that, he gets a damn good wage! I only wish he'd stop leaving those fucking calling cards in the door!"

Since this wasn't the first time I had heard Ted's suspicions about Athena's imagined suitors, I discharged them as the natural paranoia which was so much a part of him. Of course, I'd already gleaned Pickett's infatuation with Athena. But halfway through his second martini, Ted began to calm down—and on a ninety-proof high, turned the conversation to loftier things.

"Do you believe in God?"

"Sometimes," I said.

"Christ, nobody believes in God anymore."

"It's God or money," I said.

His eyes fixed on me. "You don't like our time—do you, Brooke?" he said.

"It's the only time we've got."

"That doesn't answer my question. You don't like this Yuppie generation."

"It scares me," I admitted.

"What does a guy like you have to be afraid of?"

"That no one's in charge."

"If anyone's in charge, it's you and me," he said.

"That's what I'm afraid of."

"There's never been anyone better," he said.

"So, 'Greed is good'?"

"Whoever said it, almost had it right."

"Almost..." I repeated.

"The only thing he missed is, some are better at it than others."

"So, where does it end?"

"That's the beauty of it! It ends with the last man standing!"

"I wonder who that is," I sarcastically rejoined.

He grinned. "You're looking at him."

During lunch, Ted's hostile edge began to dull, and by his second espresso, he had assumed a magnanimity toward almost everything we talked about. This was a trait I admired in him—the capacity to let go of a bad mood. In the spirit of keeping the peace, I followed suit, letting go of my own.

"Brooke," he said, exuding satisfaction, "I think you need a woman."

"You noticed," I complained.

"And I'm told—" he intoned the singsong quality of a tattletale, "you were quite a lady's man at Yale!"

I had a good idea who Ted's mole had been—a Big Man on Campus-type from Greenwich, who never forgave me for being asked to a Whiffenpoof bash by a girl he was pursuing.

"Strasberger?" I asked.

"Yeah," he said. "He still can't figure it out."

"It was his hometown. She hated Greenwich. We were natural allies."

"Anyway," Ted said, ignoring the dig, "do I have a woman for you. Tapley Sweeney—ever hear of her?"

"No," I said, getting nervous. Not that I wasn't intrigued by the prospect of a woman in my life again. It was the source of the proposal I was worried about—that smelled more like a proposition.

"Beautiful chick, Brooke—beautiful. And when I say beautiful, I mean beautiful. Her father's Franklin Sweeney.

Sweeney Computer—I'm sure you know the firm. Tapley moved to Newport after us," he said, leaning back in his chair. Then, stretching a smile and drawing in a breath, he sighed, "as a good place to play with Daddy's millions."

Before I could express my reticence, Ted forcefully went on, "But shit—she says she's going to leave Newport if her social life doesn't pick up. I'd hate to see her leave, Brooke. She's such a great girl. So, I thought we'd have you both for dinner."

I thanked him for the thought—before he came back with an all too definite date. At a loss for what to say, and thinking it would be an opportunity to see Athena, I carelessly agreed to what I guessed would be at least an entertaining encounter. As we shook hands in the lobby, Ted grinned again in his inimitably snide sort of way, and for the first time, I noticed he had a significant space between his two front teeth. "I knew you were a lady's man," he said. "For Christ's sake, Brooke, I just knew it."

It had been unbearably hot all week, a New England phenomenon euphemistically called Indian Summer—that late spell of stifling heat that comes every September, leaving its casualties gasping for air and breathless indignation. When I left the house at 7, the mercury was hovering above ninety degrees. And by the time I reached the Talbots' driveway, my suit was drenched in sweat.

As I left my car and started for the house, a red Jag was parked at the door. The top was down, and standing on the passenger seat lurched a Doberman Pinscher, leashed to the steering wheel and territorially snarling at the intruder. Arriving at the door, I saw Ted through the screen, pacing the foyer floor.

I considered retreating to make another entrance—this time whistling as I came—but he caught sight of me and rushed to the door, opening the screen. I had never seen him in a tie before. He was wearing his crested Hall of Fame blazer and light-weight khaki pants; I couldn't help but notice, above his tassel loafers, that he wasn't wearing socks.

"Brooke! Come in!" he loudly announced—as if surprised that I was paying a visit.

In unprecedented form, he reached out his hand, and obediently I shook it—then led me across the entry floor toward the back of the house. Athena was leaning against a sunroom window in a strapless seersucker dress. Offering a smile, and her slender collarbone, she outshone the setting sun.

"Where's Tapley?" Ted demanded, seeming agitated.

"Out counting sailboats. Hello, Brooke!"

As Ted disappeared, Athena stared at me from across the solarium. It could have been light, but as she stared, she looked like she was going to cry. Perhaps she was embarrassed by being so admired and came forward as a last defense—the lingering sadness on her lower lip made me want to kiss them both to tenderness.

"I've missed you, Brooke!" she said. "How are you?"

"Curious," I said.

"Don't be," she replied. "As they say in Hollywood, you've seen this movie before."

She conveyed a knowing look, and I turned to see Ted with a woman in tow behind him. "Brooke," Ted announced, with the earnestness of an overwrought adolescent, "I would like you to meet—Tapley Sweeney!"

A full bronzed face floated from behind Ted's shoulder. She was moderately attractive—though I was never one for the brass of peroxided hair. Her heavy eyes managed to look down on me despite their inferior height; and when she blinked, I thought how her eyelids stayed closed just a moment too long.

"How do you do?" she condescendingly remarked, holding out a listless hand.

"It's nice to meet you," I exaggerated, in deference to our beaming host.

"Ted has gone *on* and *on*," she said.

Where Ted had gone, I wasn't sure.

Her speech was stuffy and affected, drawing out each syllable as though it would be her last. It had a quality that my aunt used to say one only hears in the offspring of middle-class parents who suddenly find themselves with a lot of money and no way to erase the past. She referred to it as 'Locust Valley Lock-Jaw'—an orthopedic condition attributed to that Long Island watering hole for those who had so found their fortune—and I was amused to discover the Sweeneys had migrated to this strange stretch of desperate promise east of New York, if not to Locust Valley itself.

I watched her mouth default to its pursed position. By her cheeks, I had to wonder if someone had slipped her a slice of cocktail lemon. In spite of my hunch that she probably didn't have a sense of humor, I hoped that at least she might appreciate my penchant for cynicism.

A tray of gin and tonics materialized. As Tapley sashayed toward the waiting tray, I realized she was one of those strong-hipped girls who might one day be fat.

Plucking a drink, she paraded about the steamy solarium as though she'd been asked to model the latest suburban warm-weather line.

At this late date, she was still wearing a white cotton sundress—with a boldly striped one-piece bathing suit making itself known underneath. Her sun-streaked hair was tightly pulled back and tied with a white silk scarf. "A beautiful blonde," my aunt loved to refrain, "too bad she dyes her roots black."

Serenely withdrawn at the dinner table as only she could be, Athena reigned as a last enlightened outpost in an otherwise troubled world. Sphinx-like, she peered from across the table as though she knew something I didn't—only intensifying my desire to have her sitting next to me. But her presence was enough, however distanced by the vacuous conversation, freeing me to turn to Tapley and ask, "How did you come to Newport?"

"Daddy thought I needed a rest after New York. I was a headhunter there for two years, Brooke. So, he bought me a condo in Brewster Cottage, and I've been here ever since."

"Tap lives in the Yuppie ghetto, Brooke."

She indignantly turned to Ted. "And how are you any different," she said, "except that you have more money?"

Ted grinned—as if about to serve match point. "That I have more money," he said.

"Do you like it?" I attempted to mediate.

"How time drags when you're bored to death! I can't *believe* I left the city. I had this absolutely *terrific* job with the biggest agency in Manhattan! But," she winked, picking up her drink, "what's good for Daddy is good for Tap!"

As she raised the glass, an avalanche of gold bracelets fell to her elbow. "I knew some terrific fellows there. And some really great gals. Oh, God, it was *fabulous*! I had a *smashing* time! Daddies can be *so* silly sometimes!"

For the first time she smiled, revealing a row of astonishingly white front teeth.

"Do you think you'll go back?" I hopefully asked.

"God knows, Brooke," she bemoaned. "I've told Mummy and Daddy what a *morgue* it is up here. But Mummy just keeps telling me it 'builds character'. So here I am, building character!"

"And how are you doing?" Athena asked from behind her water goblet.

Apparently affronted by the question, she replied, "Better than most."

"I'm sure you would agree," Athena retorted, "in Newport, it isn't hard to do."

"What's wrong with Newport?" Ted reacted. "It beats the hell out of New York!"

"Most of New York," Tapley allowed. "But I didn't live in most of New York."

"Brooke, what do you think?" Athena said, turning and grinning at me. Her elbow was planted on the linen tablecloth, and her chin, in the palm of her hand. I wanted to kick her under the table, but her ankle was out of reach.

"About what?" I asked.

"About character," she said, continuing to grin.

I hesitated. "From what I can tell, you either have it or you don't."

I gleaned from the ensuing conversation that Tapley had gone to Vassar, which in light of what was happening to 'higher education', I wasn't surprised to hear. For this was a time when private colleges accepted anyone who could afford them—offering their students upper-class insurance in lieu of the liberal arts. In my mind, I had her in riding boots, sitting in a verse-writing course, penning bad poetry and driving an over-qualified professor insane.

Following the fifth 'fabulous', and third 'gorgeous' and 'superb', it was clear to the room that Tapley and I were probably not meant to be. I was feeling a bit uncomfortable, knowing Ted's hopes for my performance, and so was relieved when I glimpsed Athena comically roll her eyes. When Tapley brought up yet again the accomplishments of Daddy, Athena disappeared and returned with a server and the first course of cocktail shrimp.

Before Athena could raise her fork, Tapley randomly announced, "Speaking of dreadful experiences—" She awaited the table's attention. "I was accosted by one of your yachtsmen on his schooner last week! Can you imagine? Taking advantage of a woman on the wide-open sea?"

Clearly unnerved by the unfolding story, and with several shrimp on his fork, Ted aimed the instrument in Tapley's direction and desperately inquired, "What happened?"

"I told him I had tuberculosis!" she said, beginning to giggle.

Launching an exaggerated fit of laughter, Ted pushed away from the table—dramatically repeating over and over to himself, "Tuberculosis!"

Athena glanced at me.

"So, what did he do?" Ted histrionically wheezed.

"He came about, tacked to shore, and raced to the hospital!"

Lost in the hilarity of the moment, Ted blustered. "Yachtsmen are pigs!"

"Oh, come now, Ted," Tapley contested. "They're better than tennis players."

"Boats are dirty," Ted declared. "All that drug-running from Colombia to Key West? That all has to do with the sailboats."

"I thought those were cigarette boats," Tapley skeptically intoned.

"It's in all the magazines," Ted explained, dismissing inconvenient fact.

"Not in Brooke's magazine," Athena bantered, smiling across at me.

"Brooke knows what I mean," Ted graciously pronounced on my behalf. "Don't you, Brooke?"

Tapley was well into her third Chardonnay when she fawningly turned to Ted. "You certainly know about the nasty side of tennis. Who could forget the explosive tennis ball you planted on the number two seed at the French Open?"

Ted looked around the table with as much embarrassment as his calculating motive could muster. "Those were the good old days," he boasted. "Those days are all but gone."

"The problem with tennis," Tapley grieved, "is its *accessibility*. I mean, *anyone* can play. There must be public courts in every town in the country!"

"That isn't real tennis," Ted rescued privilege. "Hacks that start on public courts never leave. The best still come from the private clubs—even in the communist countries."

"I don't know," she dubiously sighed. "It's just become such a—*public* sport."

"What's wrong with that?" I outlived my welcome.

Silence bloomed in the room. Following a pause I could have cut with my knife, Tapley slowly turned her head—and fluttered her eyelids with such indignation that I thought they were going to fly off.

"Brooke—" she reflected, wincing with the concentration of a mathematician. Then, as if searching for just the right word, she observed, "We're not—hitting it off."

"Brooke didn't mean that, did you, Brooke?" Ted raced to my defense. "What's wrong with that!" he chuckled to himself, acknowledging my faux pas. "Hell, Brooke has more breeding than all of us put together—don't you, Brooke? You've been in more goddam private clubs than anyone at this table!"

"No," Tapley declined Ted's valiant attempt, "I have to say—I know Brooke's type. Brooke is the high and mighty—*moral* type." She deliberately turned to Ted. "The last single man in Newport," she exhaustedly regretted, "and we don't get along."

"Brooke is great—I'll give him that," Ted prepared to throw me under the bus. "But there are plenty of other young bachelors around!"

"Who?" Tapley asked.

With a sardonic grin, Athena replied, "The only one I know is Father Pickett."

Ted burst into alcoholic approval for Athena's ironic remark.

"What's so funny?" Tapley inquired.

Ted bellowed, "He's a goddam priest!"

"Is he celibate?" she asked.

Ted bellowed again. "As far as I can tell!"

"Is he *Catholic*?" she queried.

"No—" Athena said, sending a chill into the room.

"Then what's so funny?" Tapley came back. "Besides, I've never *had* a priest."

I had the feeling we were readying for a bell-ringing storm—Ted, seething at the thought that a woman like Tapley would consider a lowly cleric, and Athena, regretting what she had intended as at most a defiant quip.

"Tapley, he's a goddam priest!" Ted hollered. "And for Christ's sake, a poor one at that!"

"What do I care about his finances?" Tapley waxed egalitarian. "God, *having* a priest would certainly be better than *being* a nun."

Athena's face was flushed.

"Is he an Episcopal priest?"

"He is," Ted begrudgingly imparted.

"I mean, Episcopal priests *do* it—don't they?"

Suddenly, Ted looked nervous.

"Is he handsome?" she persisted.

Athena looked away.

"Then I would like to meet him."

A resounding crack broke from the far end of the table. Athena was standing before the shattered remains of an elegant dinner plate. However intimidating Ted could be, I suspected she had even frightened Ted. "You're a bully!"

Athena bitterly raged, "And one day you'll be sorry!" She glared at Tapley. "You'll both be sorry! We'll all be sorry one day!" With that, she swept out of the room and into the hot summer night.

Tapley wearily asked Ted for a drink. It was clear she didn't want to talk to me, and that even drunk, Ted was embarrassed. Having had enough, I excused myself and went out in search of Athena.

The lawn was aglitter with the evening dew, like a shimmering field of diamonds. The moon was almost full, save a depression toward the top as though an angel's finger pressed it there, and I wondered if it was growing to round perfection, or receding into darkness. All I knew for sure was, for the first time that night, I felt free to breathe again.

As I walked down from the house, I felt the seasons turn. It didn't come on a cold wind, or a falling leaf, but in that scent released somewhere from the ground or a fall garden which tells you that the end is near. For in that instant, you are given the gift for which you waited the year—of bringing back every sweet sad tragedy of love that ever crossed your path, and turning its pain into a glimmering wake of the magnificent lives you once led.

Athena wasn't on the Cliff Walk as I had thought. Turning back from the pounding sea, I saw her descending the lawn. She was startled when I appeared to her out of the dark, but wiping her eyes with the back of her wrist, she bade me a polite, "Hello."

"Are you alright?" I asked her.

"I'm alright," she said. Her dulcet voice tremored—before a single tear rolled onto her moon-bathed cheek. "It was just a joke."

"What was?" I asked.

She couldn't bring herself to speak. "He's—a priest," she wept, looking up at me. "He's just a priest—who remembers the past."

If I loved her then, with the world we once shared, I knew that neither would return. The truth was, we had met when we were too young. Like distant cousins who are vaguely aware of one another's existence, a line had been drawn that made confessions of love impossible.

And what we knew between us, we couldn't say out loud—that Pickett was bringing it back. This mystifying priest, that neither of us knew had been guarding the garden wall, was emerging from the dim of a forgotten past to dwell in the light of the day. Though she was born to circumstances Pickett was not, and only later could have imagined, he had reached back and touched a young girl's heart, and reclaimed a world that was gone.

She must have believed that it was over —love, romance, a young girl's hopes in this aimless, hopeless time. Before her had been a panacea, sold by the young entrepreneurs, who promised the world and failed to deliver more than a dead man's dreams. And then, as if by chance, she unexpectedly encountered something she had loved and lost, and found amid the ashes of a dying age, undying traces of her destiny.

I put my arm around her shoulder and walked her back to the house. It was as though, in that fleeting meeting on the lawn, I was given a forbidden glimpse of some tragic sensitivity with which she was born, and must have raged in her as a child. As far as Athena seemed to have come from Elizabeth's devastated life—and impervious as she had always appeared to the casualties of romance—I was sobered by the ineluctable fact that no matter how far we come, we are never far enough from the inevitable truth that life is a mortal condition.

As we entered the dining room, a server from the pantry asked to speak with Athena. When she didn't return, I took a stroll in search of Ted and Tapley, finally landing in a distant living room, where they were nowhere to be seen. Several minutes later, I heard footsteps on what I guessed was a servant's staircase—concealed behind the mahogany-paneled wall that was facing me.

When the hidden door opened, Tapley appeared, immediately followed by Ted. "Brooke!" Ted exclaimed. "There you are!"

"Here I am," I said.

"Where's Athena?"

"I'm not sure," I said. "I left her in the dining room."

"What a beautiful night! Did you go out?"

"Yes," I said. "Did you?"

In a vaudevillian moment, the instant Ted said "Yes!", Tapley tolled a resounding, "No!"

Ted's face was scarlet. "We were out—on the terrace! That's a tricky question!"

Ted's plea sent Tapley into hysterics—before I granted him that, inside or out, it was certainly a lovely night.

"Brooke," Ted considered, turning from Tapley, "I've done some thinking—since dinner. I don't think it would be such a bad idea to have Tapley meet Father Pickett."

Unpredicted as this was, I knew Ted well enough to detect an impending request.

"And I was wondering if you'd get in touch with him for us—I mean, of course, for Tapley!"

Desperate to avoid further involvement, I explained I hadn't seen him in a while.

"And I thought we could meet at the Hunt Club," Ted suggested.

"With Athena?" I came back.

Ted looked at me as though my mind were in the gutter. "Christ, Brooke, Athena is my wife!"

If in retrospect it is painfully clear that I should have declined the request, those were desperate, dizzying days, when I lacked my better judgment. It wasn't that I believed Ted Talbot was incapable of having an affair; it was that I couldn't fathom any man betraying a woman like Athena. And in the end, I would be right. Ted was as unable to live without Athena as Pickett was able to forget.

Chapter 6

In the dying days of October, when autumn fans its dazzling tail, and the cold air begins to descend from the north, one rides the days in an unsettled excitement that an end is near. Brought to a single breathless moment is the treacherous choice we must make for the beginning of every dream we have dreamed, and the end of all that would carry us there. It is the heart-rending call to live with the fate of a mortal life, as one who believes he will never die.

It was on one such crystal-blue morning of fall that I awoke to the prospect of this very strange day. I had never felt comfortable at the Hunt Club, despite being introduced in a nanny's arms, and that the Adams had belonged since my great-great-grandfather helped to found the place. I suppose it had something to do with its being a fertile incubator for such benign observations as 'That's Cam Adams' boy', and, 'What a tough one that was'.

But if the truth were known, my discomfort had more to do with a fear of horses. I had always found them to be at once magnificent and cruel—their weight, their power, their enigmatic desire to prevail. Thrilling as it was to watch a thoroughbred leaping fences like an athlete, I couldn't help but wonder if the thrill was less the spectacle of Grand Prix competition than routing for the stallion to dethrone its ruthless rider, to the end of being set free.

Yet I liked the open countryside, the deep green fields, the towering woods and understated clubhouse; I liked the equine musk and spartan locker rooms that went unchanged in a hundred years, despite perennial heretical suggestions of renovation by younger members. And I was still amused by the hunting prints I first encountered in the halls when I was five—from the red riding jackets high upon their mounts, to wild bears urinating in the wood. It was a club of hard-boiled millionaires who'd made their money 'when a buck was a buck', and where the cunning by which they had made every one would here be enshrined forever.

I didn't see Pickett's car when I arrived, though Athena's was parked at the door. Pickett had telephoned several times a day since I called with Ted's invitation—asking questions ranging from what he should wear, to where he could leave his car.

"You mentioned Athena will be there," Pickett said.

"Yes," I reassured him.

"And that it *is* the Hunt Club—not the Hall of Fame."

"Yes, the Hunt Club," I said. "In fact, I can pick you up if you like."

"Thanks, Brooke. That won't be necessary."

The Maître d' was stationed at the front door as I climbed the clubhouse steps, coming forward to impart that 'Mr. Talbot' had been expecting me. I scanned the porch before he explained that Ted was in a back field, shooting. Calling over a boy who looked too young to drive, I was chauffeured out in a Rover.

Left off at the gate, I leaned against the fence for several minutes, watching. Ted was down on one knee in field pants, his shotgun slung over the gleaming fender of a black Mercedes Benz, shattering clay pigeons into the forest ahead while a man in a white coat stationed next to him released them into the sky. As a one-time skeet-shooter myself, I knew a good one when I saw one—and Ted was good.

When he had emptied the box of shells on the trunk, I called out to him. He turned and waved, dismissed his man, and came striding toward me with the gun. Like everything he owned, it was a beautiful gun—a Beretta over-and-under—broken and braced under his arm as though it were a part of him.

"That's what I like about it!" he shouted. "The pigeons always lose!"

I gripped his outstretched hand.

"Everybody here?"

"I don't know," I told him.

"The parson?" he asked, looking at me as if he were about to laugh.

I shrugged, in hopes of absolving myself of any responsibility.

"Christ!" he went on, biting his lip and staring at the ground like a hawk. "I mean, this is crazy! A goddam priest! And a beautiful woman like Tapley!"

"She couldn't be considering a nicer guy."

"Who the hell's side are you on?"

"No one's," I said.

"Then you're not on mine."

"Why do you even care?"

"Christ, Brooke, Tapley is my girlfriend!" he cried.

"What?"

"Tapley's my girlfriend!"

As surely as I had seen it coming, it was nonetheless a shock. It was not the kind of shock that abruptly implodes in response to devastating news; it was the kind that overwhelms with irrevocable regret for having chosen to be naïve. If it had little to do with the perpetrator—who was just being who he was—it had everything to do with the star-crossed victim of the cards she had been dealt.

Ted slung the broken gun across his shoulder. "For Christ's sake!" he fumed, almost scolding me. "I would have thought you'd have figured that out!

"Why do you think she came to Newport!" he roared, as if I were the one to be blamed.

With a pit in my stomach as leaden as the gun, I shot back, "Does Athena know?"

"Hell, no!" he railed. "If that got out, I'd be through at the Hall—and with my sponsors! You can get away with damn near anything in tennis. Anything but cheating! I'm telling you, Brooke, I'd be blackballed forever! Goddam hypocrites!"

"Then why did you push Pickett into this?" I seethed, feeling suddenly sick.

"Tapley was going to leave! She said if I didn't find her an escort, she was going back to New York!"

"So why the hell Pickett!"

"A power thing," he groused. "She claims I call all the shots. As soon as she saw I didn't like Pickett, she would only take the priest!

"Anyway," he sighed, "I gotta figure something out. Got any ideas?"

"You wouldn't want to hear them."

"Thank God, I have a prenup."

"Thank your lawyer," I steamed.

He laughed. "Good point."

"So much for love."

"What does that mean?" he came back.

"Once you sign a prenup, it's been traded away."

"You've never been married."

"Maybe they cared too much about money."

"There's no such thing," he said.

"Then Athena will never leave."

"That's the goddam problem. Athena's the exception."

"I'd consider that a virtue."

"I mean, how the hell can you trust a woman like that?"

Athena was sitting alone on the veranda, looking out over the hunt course. Her finely fitted hunt coat opened on her breeches, and her field boots were unlaced at the ankles. Smitten as I was by her beguiling charisma, I had never taken deliberate account of the nature of Athena's beauty.

It was as though she'd been allowed to take it all for granted—her world, her place, whence she had come, and where she was destined to go. Her smile, her eyes, the freshness of her face, it seemed, would never grow old. She knew who she was, and the gifts she had been given by virtue of her birth, yet never had she gloated, nor slighted in the least those who were less than she.

I wondered if she had ever considered that life could be any different. Despite the misfortunes she had known in her past, I presumed she had escaped unscathed. Having been reared on the liberal assumption that women were nobler than men—that the feminine mystique was innately superior to masculine competition—thanks to Athena, I discovered that it wasn't gender, but a winsome spirit, which saw the futility of blind ambition in either a woman or a man.

As I greeted Athena, Tapley emerged from the clubhouse in an evening gown. Whether she'd just come from an all-night affair or was about to go to one, it was at least entertaining to watch the indignation contorting members' faces. Sitting down next to Ted with a drink, she vaguely raised her glass at Athena—who gazed at me from the other side of Ted with a fleeting look of tragedy.

And in that moment, Athena's countenance changed— as if she had become another woman. It was not that she had lost the objective beauty which any man would admire; it was that it was now an objective beauty of which I was no longer a part. Her impossible vitality, finding its fulfillment at Elizabeth's wedding in Ashfield, had etiolated from her animated face like color from a dying flower.

Stricken by dread that she knew the truth, I sat down next to her. It was as though she was unutterably alone in a world that no longer understood her. As much as I had hoped there was something to be done to redeem her untimely dreams—some miraculous phoenix, rising from the pyre of this burning, vainglorious time—in that moment, despite my puritanical scruples about the sanctity of marriage, when Pickett appeared on a distant lawn, he was no less than a glimpse of salvation.

I regretted answering Pickett's final query about standard hunt club attire. A black velvet hunt cap was tucked under his arm as he charged up the hill to the veranda. Nevertheless, he carried it off as few men could have done; in fact, as handsome as he looked, I feared the fuel that might be added to Ted's smoldering fire.

"Well, look at you," Ted sarcastically reacted.

Attempting to decipher his mocking tone, Pickett shook Ted's hand. Ted barely introduced Pickett to Tapley, who looked taken with her intended, proceeding to scrutinize him head-to-toe as he sat down next to her. "And Athena!" Pickett stood up again. "I'm sorry—I didn't see you!"

With a wisp of sadness, Athena's eyes mirrored Pickett's innocence. "It's been too long," she tenderly said. "You don't come to see me anymore."

"He still leaves those calling cards in the door!" Ted voraciously guffawed.

Pickett looked embarrassed.

"Hell," Ted went on, "we have enough to play five rounds of poker!"

"So," Tapley said, as Pickett sat again, "what's it like being a man of God?" She was playing with a long string of cultured pearls hanging loosely around her neck. "I mean, it must be awfully depressing—reading the Bible all the time!"

Pickett was about to attempt a response when Tapley weighed in again. "And all that black! I mean, it's one thing in the evening! But my God, all day long?"

Athena glanced at me with a scintillating glint that made me almost laugh—giving me to glean through the tear in her eye, a possible glimmer of hope.

"I don't know much about the church," Tapley said. "I mean, I *do* believe in God. I just don't believe I have to go to church to prove it. Do you believe I have to go to church to prove it, John? I mean, I *do* believe in God. Just not the church's God. For me, God is a great universal—*thing* in the sky! Just incredibly—*universal*!"

Taken off-guard by Tapley's unexpected theological insight, Pickett managed to endure her homilies through the rest of lunch. Ted's silence became increasingly apparent, and his face, progressively flushed. Athena was watching the three of them when she caught sight of my furtive surveillance—spontaneously leaping up from the table and pulling her chair next to mine.

"I've missed you, Brooke!" she said.

"I've missed *you*," I said.

Pickett looked instantly forlorn.

"I mean," I attempted to reassure my cohort, "I've missed our conversations."

"When are you going to fall in love, Brooke Adams?"

"When I find the right woman to love."

"I'm not the right woman?"

"You're the right woman. I'm just not the right man."

Ted got up and stormed into the clubhouse. If it wasn't anger at Athena's flirtation, it was at not being the center of attention. Ignoring his departure, and Athena's lively banter, Tapley talked on at Pickett.

As I watched Athena studying this enigmatic priest—as if she knew him better than herself—I felt suddenly, uncharacteristically, jealous of another man. I wasn't jealous because I already suspected he had won Athena's heart. I was jealous because he harbored a hope I knew I no longer had.

A great sable thoroughbred came cantering around the clubhouse with Ted high in the saddle. Its massive arching neck was already lathered in the cold October air, impatiently lunging toward the sky, and quaking the earth beneath. A second horse, almost identical to the first, came restlessly prancing behind—led on a lunge line by a stable boy who had all he could do to subdue it.

"Father!" Ted called, jostled up and down by his highly-strung mount. "You look like a horseman! Let's jump the old course! The two of us—together!"

Startled by the invitation, Pickett looked across at me—perhaps hoping I could reach into my bag of tricks and offer him a way out. "I've ridden very little!" he pleaded his case.

"Piece of cake!" Ted blustered. "We'll take the easy ones! You're the priest! All you gotta do is keep the faith!"

Receiving little more than bewilderment from me, Pickett rose from his chair. He left his riding crop on the seat, pressed his hunt cap onto his head, and, turning from Athena's evident concern, ventured down the stairs to the stirrup. The instant the stableboy raised him to the saddle, I guessed Pickett's 'very little' had probably consisted of several sunny Saturday afternoons in junior high.

As Pickett's foot was groping for the other stirrup, Ted gathered his horse underneath him, and shot off toward the hunt field with Pickett clutching the saddle at a gallop behind. Miraculously, after the first three fences he had managed to stay on top, desperately clinging onto the mane while churning up a wake. I was beginning to have a giddy confidence in Pickett's perseverance when Athena cried out, "They're headed for the bank! That hasn't been jumped in years!"

"It's a huge drop!" one of the stable hands shouted, jumping up and down beneath us.

As though she knew what was coming, Athena leapt up and ran into the clubhouse. When Ted arrived at the jump, he pulled his horse out of the approach, and with nowhere else to go, Pickett careened over the precipice into the ravine. I was off the veranda and halfway there when the horse trotted from behind the bank—the saddle was empty and turned on its girth, and the reins were hanging free.

Pickett was lying on his back in the mud, clutching his arm across his chest. His face, half-hidden by the velvet helmet, was contorted in agony.

"I trust the parson's all right!" Ted's voice jovially boomed down from his saddle.

Pickett tried to look up.

"It was all in fun, Father! All in fun!"

Pickett was in shock. Tapley was immediately kneeling at my side, helping to lift him off the ground. In characteristic fashion, she commanded a stable hand to call an ambulance.

By the time we had gotten Pickett back across the field, he appeared to be coming around. Still holding his arm, looking wildly deformed, he was deliriously mumbling to himself, "It doesn't hurt much—I don't believe it's—broken—I may need—to see a doctor."

As we climbed the stairs, Ted was on the veranda, talking to several men. He seemed to take no notice, but continued telling a story which resulted in a hearty round of laughter as we passed into the clubhouse. The table where we were dining was empty, and Athena was nowhere to be seen.

Accompanying Pickett through the clubhouse lobby, I steered him to a bench on the front porch. By the time the silenced ambulance came creeping up the drive—per order of the Master of the Club—a complement of bus boys and stable hands, encircling the two of us, were inspecting Pickett's twisted limb with morbid curiosity. Word had obviously gotten out that it was more than an accident, because when Ted appeared, in a matter of seconds, every one of them was gone.

I glared at Ted before turning back to Pickett, who was stoically getting to his feet. As painful as it must have been, I wondered how the hell he was standing. Yet for all his modesty and self-effacing decorum, there was a steely conviction in Pickett's eyes that this was not to be the end.

"You're alright," Ted gruffly remarked. "Aren't you, Father Pickett?"

At first, I thought the hurt in Pickett's eyes was that of physical pain. Then I realized that for Pickett, it was worse. It was the pain of having been betrayed.

The ambulance arrived at the clubhouse door and two attendants jumped out. Even Tapley was furious at Ted as she escorted Pickett down the stairs. I entered the back of the ambulance behind her evening gown in order to assure the ashen priest that I would see him at the hospital. "Thank you, Brooke—" he disjointedly replied, "but it's—really not necessary."

I watched the ambulance disappear down the drive, with disgust awash in my gut. When the siren sounded for the first time on the road, a chill telegraphed up my spine, despite telling myself that it was just a broken arm, and Pickett would be alright. But in that moment, I derived cold

comfort from knowing Pickett would physically recover—
that there was something which had gone far beyond Pickett
that wouldn't be made right again.

Turning to Ted, I angrily snapped, "Why the fuck did
you do it?"

"Why did I do what?"

I glared at him.

"The horse ran away with me!"

"It's never your fault—is it Ted?"

"Look, I'll pay the bill!"

"You'll pay the bill."

"That's why you're pissed."

"Tell me—why am I pissed?"

"You think I should pay the bill," he said.

"You don't have enough to pay the bill."

I drove alone to the hospital. Tapley was sitting in the
waiting room, twisting her string of pearls, and reading a
celebrity magazine as though nothing had happened. For the
first time, she was attractive to me. She'd shown a quick-
witted wisdom I imagined she used staving off the skipper
on the high seas, and as I stood in the white light of the
waiting room, I felt a flood of admiration for her.

A surgeon put Pickett back together. The nurse at the
desk summoned me to say there was a question about
insurance. I told her that Pickett was a very good friend, and
where I lived in town, and convinced her that if he wasn't
covered, I would take care of it.

Several hours later, Pickett exited through the swinging
doors—a cast and sling cradling his arm, and color returned
to his face. The mud that caked his riding coat was dry, as
was the blood on his shirt. Tapley got up and went over to

him. "Congratulations, Father Pickett! At least you're in one piece! His last opponent at the Italian Open never won a tournament again."

I asked her if she needed a ride. Considering the offer, she graciously declined. Wishing Pickett a restful night, and 'fun with all those drugs', she asked me for a quarter and went to the public telephone across the lobby.

As I drove Pickett home, with the dry October leaves flying in the autumn wind, the knot in my stomach was more than the sorrow that wells at the end of the day. It may have been the betrayal in his eyes as he was looking up at Ted—or perhaps the fear that his innocence had ended in that one fall. Whatever it was, it wasn't only Pickett who had me mourning that night; it was all of us, who had hoped for so much more, and settled for so much less.

As I opened my front door, the phone was ringing. Although I had expected Athena to call, I wasn't prepared for the deluge. "I'm sorry!" she heaved, "I just—couldn't stay! I knew this—was going to happen!"

Before I could respond, she cathartically grieved, "What has—happened to us?"

"I—don't know," I finally confessed.

"It was such—a terrible fall!"

Chapter 7

I had been out of town for a month of Sundays covering wooden boat races when Pickett caught me after the service and discreetly took me aside.

"Brooke," he said, "I have a favor to ask."

I curiously waited him out.

"I was wondering if you could come with me to New York," he said, looking embarrassed.

"I'm afraid I'm in a bit of a jam," he explained. "I've got this fundraising event for the bell tower—and I'm scheduled to go down with Tapley. To tell you the truth, I'm not entirely comfortable with Tapley, as yet."

"You're going to New York with Tapley?" I said, failing to conceal my surprise.

"Well, Ted will be with us," Pickett imparted. "But that just makes it more difficult."

"What makes it more difficult?"

"Ted's hopes for our hitting it off," he confided.

"What about Athena?"

"Athena is already there."

"When is the party?"

"Friday evening."

"The night after Thanksgiving?"

"Yes," he apologized.

I hesitated. "I'm afraid I'll be—well, maybe I can make it back."

He looked relieved. "Ted has offered the Hall of Fame's limousine."

"We can take my car," I strongly advised.

Pickett looked disappointed.

"Limousines can make you sicker than boats."

"It's not the limousine," he said.

"What is it?" I asked.

"It may be Ted's way of saying that he's sorry."

Dusk had fallen when I turned up my collar and walked out to the street. As planned, at precisely 5 o'clock, the limousine drew up to the curb. It was one of those moments when you ask yourself how you've gotten into this fix; but fully committed, I had no choice but to steel myself for the ride.

The rear compartment was illuminated, casting light onto its occupants. Ted and Tapley were engaged in a lover's quarrel of mutual pinching and tickling, producing hysterical giggles that were audible through the heavy glass. Pickett was sitting to one side on a jump seat, his long legs elegantly crossed, and peering out the window as if trying to allow the couple some privacy.

When the chauffeur opened the limousine door, a waft of Bourbon escaped. I angled my way around the bar to the unoccupied seat, facing Pickett. Brightening on my arrival, Pickett greeted me through an air of exclusion that made me wish I had prevailed in taking my car.

Pickett was wearing a black cashmere coat and an elegant white silk scarf. Checking on his injured arm, I noted an empty sleeve. The starched white cuff protruding from the other evoked the look of an admiral; and his eyes, peering with knowing delight, agreed with his mischievous smile.

Tapley's dress was daringly spare despite the November weather, baring a shoulder from a wrap of satin and a choker of exaggerated diamonds. She greeted me between cigarette puffs, and Ted offered an exhausted wave. It didn't take long to deduce that the party had started hours ago.

"I don't suppose," Ted mumbled, lifting his head off the back of his seat, "that these high-class affairs make you any too comfortable—do they, Father Pickett?"

"Why is that?" asked Pickett.

"What with a couple of bishops looking over your shoulder. But then, rich priests like you don't have to worry about their jobs, do they Pickett?

"I hear the Presiding Bishop will be there," Ted feigned an optimistic note. "I guess he only shows up for fundraisers over half a million."

By his inquisitive look, I suspected Pickett was searching for an honorable intention—contrary to my own assumption that Ted was just being an asshole.

"Father, have you met the Presiding Bishop? Well, of course you have! After all, you're the Rector of Newport! And if I've met him—surely *you* have!

"But then…" Ted droned on, letting his head flop back onto the deck. "Where the hell do you go from here? Like getting a Rolls…when you're sixteen.

"But with *your* money…" he said, his voice trailing off.

"You're drunk, dear Ted," Tapley said, slapping him on the cheek. Definitively nodding at the two of us, she pronounced, "Too drunk to talk."

By the time Tapley's hand had left Ted's face, he was already fast asleep. She reached in front of her and flicked on the television built into the bar. Lighting another cigarette, she was instantly engrossed in a game show, spraying canned applause and technicolor flashes into the close space around us.

And Pickett was lost to the enigmatic dark beyond the window glass. Because there is no city in the world like New York, its tremoring power was as deeply felt in the woods and hollows of southern Connecticut as it was in the city itself. For this was as much its unrivaled domain, and as we thundered down the Parkway, we silently took in its orgiastic promise, leading a thousand dark and elegant cars streaming back to their kingdoms.

Once I caught Pickett staring through the trees at the lighted houses of Westport. Though they looked to be modest, I couldn't help guessing how exciting they must have been to him. For this was the undoubted promised land, where those who'd made a difference had come— who, daring to risk the impossible odds, knew success would be lost or won.

My parents had owned an apartment in New York from the time before I was born, but apart from considering it after Paris, I had never given it much thought. New York was the consummate tragic hero—so to live there was to bear its arrogance, and the truth that one day it might fall. If its preeminence sparkled on the walks of Fifth Avenue north to Ninety-sixth Street, its fate lay in the trash-strewn gutters half a block west, and rickety markets across the park.

As we started crosstown, Ted woke up and began extolling the virtues of city life while making boorish, lascivious remarks at each hotel that we passed. He was in a fine mood, instructing the driver to take a turn around midtown to view the festive signs of Christmas. With the lighted tree of Rockefeller Center filling his open window, he ordered the chauffeur to stop in mid-traffic, then stuck out his head and got into a ferocious shouting match with a cabbie.

After Ted bellowed the final word, we traveled east and uptown—inhaling the scent of roasted chestnuts, burned pretzels, and diesel exhaust. Light snow was falling on Madison, dancing like crystal on the glass, and making magic of the swank galleries that lined the Seventies. But by the time we reached the appointed canopy and white-gloved doorman on Park, even I was feeling seasick and ready to get out of the car.

The event was already underway. By right, the Bishop of New York maintained a twenty-room house on the Cathedral close, but from the start of his episcopate, Edmond Winston chose to live in his Park Avenue coop. As a devotee of historic churches, the fundraiser was Winston's idea; and although it was Pickett who'd invited me, we knew one another from the past.

As he greeted me, I noted Winston's upper lip retained its mildly sneering quality—as though perpetually considering the utter injustice of any such notion as an inheritance tax. He showed little interest in Pickett, but came to life at Ted's erratic entrance. Within seconds, he was slapping 'Tizzy' on the back and thanking him for coming, before loudly reminiscing with 'my doubles partner' about their win at the Athletic Club.

Through pipe smoke, I captured Athena's face in the corner of the living room, encircled by a klatch of Princetonians in bow ties and banking suits. Two of them were leaning on a grand piano, flanking her on either side, and giving the impression that at any moment they were sure to break out into song. Athena was brilliantly ignoring them both with her chin propped up on a hand—gazing about in a black velvet dress as though she owned the place.

Their suspenders, starched shirts, short clipped hair, and tight, smug, red-lipped smiles gave me to ask how different we were from our silver-haired counterparts here. I wondered when it was that we had sacrificed our hopes— our loves, our dreams, our plans, and our schemes that had once made it all worthwhile. And I realized it wasn't a matter of age that determined the life we would live, but a spirit that could take us beyond our time, and give us to hope again.

As we surrendered our coats, Ted led us to the bar as though the drinks were on him. Securing three Scotches, he led us back into the middle of the room. Not surprisingly for Park Avenue, the coop was bedecked with marble-topped furnishings gilded to within an inch of their lives.

"The bishop tells me we have half the five-hundred-thousand for the belltower!" Ted announced. He thwacked Pickett's chest with the back of his hand. "That otta' make you feel pretty good, Father! After all, it's *your* church!"

Noticing that Pickett didn't have a drink, I went over to the bar and got one. He thanked me, and with his able arm, engineered a sip. Ted rapidly tired of our company, scanning the living room—and locating Athena, took Tapley's hand and disappeared through the crowd.

I pressed Pickett in Athena's direction. Looking up in a flood of surprise, she called across the piano, circumnavigating her wide-eyed suitors and leaving them behind. "And Father Pickett!" she said, unabashedly charmed, "in your dashing collar!"

The din of the crowd suddenly quelled, as all eyes turned to the bishop. "If you will indulge me—yet one more time!" Winston jauntily bellowed. "Clarence Hedgerow has just generously agreed to twenty-five thousand dollars! On behalf of the church, and in the name of God, Clarence, I give you thanks!" The crowd applauded. "Might I note," he added, "we are more than halfway there!"

"Wouldn't it be heaven to be rid of the rich?" Athena blithely remarked.

Pickett looked confounded. In an attempt to resolve his puzzlement, I challenged our dissident. "I must say," I teased, "that's a bit surprising, coming from the Princess of Newport."

"Oh, I believe in princes!" Athena laughed. "I just don't believe in the rich."

"Do you know—any princes?" Pickett asked.

She grinned. "I do," she said.

When she intimated a trip to 'freshen up', I decided to follow suit. Pickett offered to 'freshen up our drinks', and precariously left with the glasses. Making our way through the multitude to the back of the living room, I deferred to Athena, who went ahead into the powder room.

Studying an ostentatious clock on a credenza in the hall, I became aware of a muffled commotion in the bedroom behind me. When I turned around, there was Ted—drunkenly sprawled out on the bed—with Tapley frantically zipping up her dress before the righteous gaze of Bishop Winston. Hoping beyond hope that Athena was still sequestered in the powder room, I felt a hand on my shoulder and turned to see Athena's beautiful face.

"I believe in princes," she said in a whisper. "I only believe in princes."

Before I could respond, she fled down the hall and across the living room. Obstructed from making my way through the crowd, I watched her standing in the foyer as a bewildered Pickett attempted to open the door with three lowball glasses. Hearing Ted's laugh, I turned to see the bishop's arm around his shoulder; and by the time I looked back, the front door was closed and Athena and Pickett were gone.

"May I have your attention," Winston called, "for I am joyful to say, a final time! I would like to announce that none other than Ted Talbot—three-time Wimbledon champion, four-time champion of the U.S. Open—has, in an impossibly generous gesture, donated the last $200,000 to the Bell Tower Fund. The money is raised!"

Polite applause freely gave way to shrill grandstand whistles.

"Where's Athena?" Ted's voice boomed in my ear.

I wheeled around. "She's gone."

"Christ, I'll be in the city tonight. You can take my car home."

"Where is it?" I fumed.

"At Columbia—" he yawned. "I'll call it down."

"Don't bother."

Getting my coat, I noticed Pickett's, marked with the white silk scarf, and seized them both with a sense of relief at stealing them from this place. Everything I hated about this time, I had conveniently blamed on Ted. I realized then that I was one of them, one of a whole generation, who had given up our hopes as the folly of youth for the sake of our privileged places.

If I detested their style and self-satisfied smiles, I shared in their complacent ways—and gasping for air, the choice was either to leave or to suffocate. I brushed past our host as he gleefully greeted the arriving Presiding Bishop. I couldn't remember when the out-of-doors brought such a sense of liberation; and virtually rejoicing in my narrow escape, I hailed a cab for Morningside Heights.

Passing through the iron gates at 116th and Broadway, I traversed College Walk toward the long black coach in the inner sanctum of the campus. Columbia too belonged to the all-important club known as the 'Ivy League'—that understood bastion of higher learning which no one seemed to understand—yet it lacked the Jeffersonian purity one equates with pretentious institutions, bringing to bear everything it had on the greatest city in the world. As my steps broke and echoed against the great granite edifices, perched like Greek Gods in the dark, as hard as it was to imagine Ted here, it was not hard to imagine Pickett.

Rolling across the deserted campus on this Thanksgiving break, I glimpsed a lone illuminated window high on a dormitory roof. I imagined a young Pickett in the gabled room, with no home to return to, dreaming and redeeming adolescent schemes that would bear him to his destiny. I wondered if he'd known that he would be a priest—which none of us had ever thought to be—betting his life on the long odds of God instead of die a mediocre man.

I thought about my years after graduation, writing for the paper by day, and searching by night for my elusive fate, somewhere on the Champs-Élysées. Instead of working, striving, risking my life in that magical city of light, I expected it to waft from posh perfumeries as though it were my right. Pickett must have known what I had never known by virtue of his desperation—that only by the longing of so humble a life could he realize so great a destiny.

I was still in bed when the frantic knocking sounded on my front door. Opening my eyes to the sun-filled room, I was embarrassed to find it was late morning. I had barely cracked the door when Ted burst through and started pacing the living room. "They said she left with Pickett! I *knew* he had a thing for her! Even at *Columbia,* goddam it!"

"What happened to Tapley?" I blearily queried.

"I swear to God, I'll *kill* him!"

He was pounding his fist into the other hand before he returned to my question. "Christ, Brooke—I don't love *Tapley*!" he said, as if I were an idiot. "Tapley's just a girlfriend! I love *Athena*! I swear to God, I've loved her from the minute I saw her—and I swear to God I always will!"

"Pickett never talks about Athena," I fibbed.

"You'd trust a guy like Pickett?"

"Yes, I would."

"You're a nice guy, Brooke. But you know where nice guys finish."

On the Wednesday following the evening in New York, I was out for a walk on Ocean Drive when I saw Athena's car being towed past my house behind a truck from Connecticut. Phoning her twice, I twice got Ted, both times hanging up the phone. I still had Pickett's topcoat and scarf—and the need to look in on him—but it seemed so quiet on the far side of the street that I hesitated to visit.

It wasn't until deeper into the month, and I was thinking about leaving for Christmas, that I screwed up my courage one late afternoon and went over to Pickett's place. I was about to knock when I heard Athena's voice tremoring behind the door. "You don't understand! What's past is—past!"

The silence was deafening.

"No," Pickett said, with unequivocal conviction. "The past will always come back."

"How—can you *say* that?" Athena implored.

"Because it's the truth," Pickett said.

"The past will never come back!" she sobbed. This time, the silence went longer.

"Then I have failed," he solemnly pronounced.

"What—have you failed?" she pleaded.

"I've failed the truth."

"Then I'm the one who failed!"

"That's not possible," he said.

Having overstayed my unextended welcome, I quietly stole down the stairs. From inside the door came Athena's mournful cry, "If only you didn't remember!"

The next day, I returned with Pickett's coat and scarf. Happy to see me, he graciously invited me into his spartan quarters. I agreed to a beer, but before I could sit, the telephone rang in the kitchen.

"Yes," he said, "this is John Pickett." The kitchen door turned on its hinges. I picked up a magazine and noisily flipped through it, producing as much din as I could. "I'd like to place an option for two hundred thousand. Yes—for sixty days."

In the interest of Pickett's privacy, I retired to the bathroom. Closing the door, my eye went to a photograph hanging on the wall. I admired the manse before I recognized it as the Bishop's House in Providence.

What looked to be a yearbook was lying on a radiator next to the porcelain sink. I wasn't surprised to discover the name of the school from which it had come. Thanks to the memory of the tired binding, the yearbook flopped open in my hands—to a captivating black and white portrait of none other than Athena Van Fleet.

When I detected Pickett's conversation winding up, I exited the bathroom.

"You brought my coat!" he greeted me.

"I'm sorry I haven't been to church. You would have had it sooner. The last time I was there," I led the witness, "I believe you weren't."

"Thanksgiving weekend!" Pickett recalled. "I had a colleague stand in!"

"I'm glad you had a break."

"Connecticut is a beautiful state!" he offered.

"It is," I agreed.

"We found—" he hesitated. "The most wonderful—country inn!"

Before I could respond, he went back to the kitchen and returned with two bottles of beer. "I'd offer you a glass," he apologized. "But I'm a bit under-equipped."

"I prefer a bottle," I tried to reassure him.

He laughed. "I prefer a glass! My dad worked at the Narragansett Brewery—not very far from here! He always said that drinking from a glass helps to better taste the beer!"

Handing me a bottle, he invited me to sit on his shabby, oversized sofa. When he perched on an arm, I sat down on the other and observed this unassuming priest. He was wearing a white cotton collarless shirt, punctuated by redundant collar studs, and stripped of a clerical vest that was lying face-down on the back of the couch.

French cuffs, less a pair of missing links, were rolled up from his wrists, exposing virile, muscular forearms I probably wouldn't have predicted. I wondered if his injured arm had miraculously healed in my absence, or whether the undoubted surgical scars were simply hidden from view. His evident calm, which starkly contradicted his audible distress the day before—when he tragically confessed how he had failed everything he cared about—conveyed an utter self-confidence I hadn't seen before, giving me to sense that whatever lay ahead, he knew where he was going.

"So, how are you liking the job?" I asked.

"Fine, Brooke. Thanks," he said. He took a frothy sip. "It's certainly very different from what I'm used to."

"Did you get anywhere with the newspaper project?"

He smiled. "Not yet!" he said.

"I heard you didn't get very far with the vestry."

"Ted wasn't a fan," he said.

"I suspect it wasn't only Ted," I said.

"I suspect you're right," he said.

"What would it take to get the project going?"

"They say, all it takes is money."

"What would you say?"

He smiled again. "Money is never all it takes."

Before I left for Boston, I passed by the apartment to wish Pickett a Merry Christmas. He wasn't at home, so I dropped off the gift inside the building door—a photographic history of the Newport mansions and a check from his mythical patron. On my way out of town, I stopped at the Talbots in hopes of seeing Athena, but it appeared that they had already left for their annual sojourn to the Alps.

Except for a twelve-hour stopover to pack, I wasn't in Newport for a month. Having exhausted another storied week of 'An American in Paris'—our valiant post-college journalistic effort that now verged on the apocryphal—the reunion broke up, disbanding for New York, Chicago and San Francisco, while I went south to the Virgin Islands to cover a tall ship regatta. As much as I disliked the Caribbean for its sun-soaked gluttony, I decided to stay on to entertain my future out of the winter chill.

February was bitterly cold that year, keeping us all before the fire. I saw Athena several times at parties, but only for a moment before Ted steered her away in a newly solicitous fashion. He'd stopped inviting me to lunch, and seemed evasive whenever we happened to meet.

It was not until late March when I finally saw Athena without Ted. She was getting off a train from Boston as I was about to get on, and Elizabeth, donning a long black cape, was magnificently behind her. Athena recognized me through the falling snow, dancing on the railway platform—catching, twinkling above her eyes like a crystalline tiara in her hair.

"I've missed you, Brooke!" she said. "What have you been up to?"

"Trying to stay warm!" I said.

"We haven't been to church in months. Have you?"

"Several times—at eight."

"How was it?" she asked—then laughed at herself. "I mean, how was Father Pickett?"

"I didn't have a chance to speak with him," I said. "But from what I could tell, he was fine."

"Pickett loves Athena," Elizabeth said, coming to Athena's side.

"Elizabeth!" Athena scolded her.

"It's true," Elizabeth said. "Pickett has always loved Athena. And he always will."

"It's good to see you, Elizabeth," I said.

"It's nice to see you, Brooke," she replied.

Her open cashmere hood framed her lovely face and flowed into the elegant cloak. Snow was melting on her slender nose as her penetrating eyes bore down on me.

"How—is your husband?" I attempted to retreat.

"Divorced," Elizabeth said.

"Well, then—how are you?"

"Divorced," she said.

"I'm not!" Athena laughed.

"You will be," Elizabeth sternly came back.

"Elizabeth!" Athena said.

"The tennis player never loved you," she said. "Only John Pickett loves you."

"It doesn't matter—Elizabeth!" Athena said.

"It does," Elizabeth replied.

"No, it doesn't!"

"Yes, it does. Love is the only thing that matters."

As we said goodbye and I boarded the train, I found myself thinking about Pickett. However cordial he had been at the church door, something had changed between us. It was not that he seemed any less friendly than he had been before, but that he somehow appeared inscrutably distracted by an infinitely vaster landscape. It was as though he needed to conserve his energy required to take him there—still, whatever it was, and wherever he would go, I wanted to go with him.

The light burned faithfully in Pickett's upstairs window past the Ides of March, bearing me through the lingering winter to the possibility of spring. Whenever I was home, the light was the only sign that Pickett was there. Yet each time I returned, I couldn't help but imagine this enigmatic priest, churning dreams in a romantic loneliness I sensed he had always known.

Nevertheless, as I looked across the street, there was something in that faithful light that made me believe a wonderful thing could happen at any time. It may have been the promise of spring, and the second chance at love it brings. Or it may have been the sense one had about John Pickett himself.

Chapter 8

Though there had long been rumors that Rosecliff was sold—even lent credence from time to time by trucks and men lingering about the great façade of the place—each time they proved to be empty hopes of idle romantic minds that didn't have the heart or the will to dispel the vicarious claims. But it was overhearing an exchange between two ladies on the train from New York, which gave me to believe, for all the false starts, that this time it was different.

"I heard it was family money. But I don't know—" came the first provocative remark.

"They say he's from the south somewhere. An old Southern family is what I heard."

"A newspaper magnate is what I was told. Though it all sounds fishy to me."

"If he weren't a clergyman, I might believe it. But who hears of wealthy clerics anymore? That went out with our generation, Mildred. As far as I can see, these days they go into it for the uniform."

The Hall of Fame gossip was little different. While dining alone, sparing myself the misery of my own cooking, I overheard the first of the scandalous versions of the story. In a place where life began at forty, three upstarts in their thirties were engaged in lively speculation about how it could have happened.

"It's either drugs or insider trading," the first one hazarded a guess.

"It has to be drugs," the second one said. "No one's heard of his family."

"It could be syndicate money," said the third.

The second one laughed out loud. "If it is," he said, "playing a priest is one helluva cover!"

"If that's what it takes to buy Rosecliff," cracked the first, "I'd be ordained in a New York minute!"

The following morning, a Goodwill truck pulled up to the Rexall drugstore and was swiftly filled with the familiar contents of Pickett's upstairs apartment. I tried to pry loose some information from the distracted driver. But all he was able to tell me was that the tenant was not at home.

Rumors continued to roll across the sweeping stretches of Newport until the name 'John Pickett' was spoken as though the man were a God-given hero. Heretofore, no one had known who he was, or whence he could have come. But now it didn't matter to them, for all they seemed to care was this mysterious priest had brought back a lost age of magnificence.

Within a week, I received a telephone call from a resonant baritone, who brilliantly fulfilled the caricature of a Newport butler. "Mr. Pickett," he began, stripping his boss of his Episcopal ordination, "requests the honor of your presence for a cocktail—at Rosecliff," he announced.

Awaiting the details, I realized this was all he was planning to say.

"Sorry," I said, "but could you tell me when?"

He indignantly replied, "Why—now!"

The gates were closed against the setting sun, so I parked outside and started up the long winding drive on foot. Though it was after six, gardeners toiled in the gardens that had fallen to ruin—parading back and forth to a formidable truck laden with pallets of roses. When I arrived at the great neoclassical door, I was let in by a gentleman whose spare mustache and evident impatience matched the voice on the phone.

Imparting that 'the Master' was in the ballroom, the butler disappeared, leaving me in the foyer before the legendary heart-shaped staircase. On either side stood statues of Dante and Diana, while in front of me climbed a crimson carpet that looked ready for replacement. The white Carrera marble floor appeared to be freshly washed, and at the far end of the ballroom, a uniformed domestic traversed with a bucket and mop.

The ballroom was filled with spring's twilight, slanting through the windows to the sea, and gilding the air with a golden reminiscence of how it used to be. I felt almost mournful that this breathtaking place had so long been kept from the world. For decades, it had sat like a glorious tomb that wished to be remembered; yet now, by the miracle of this April night, it had come to life again.

At first, I didn't see the slender profile at the base of the towering wall, but as he stepped into the window light, I knew it had to be Pickett. "Thirty-two, thirty-three, and a third!" he paced, kicking the distant wall, and sending a sonorous bang across the vast and gleaming floor. Turning around, and searching through the shadows in my direction, he called out, "One hundred feet to the inch! They sure knew how to build them—welcome, Brooke!"

"I thought only historical societies bought houses like this!"

"They waited too long!" he called again, striding energetically toward me.

"Are you really going to live here?" I incredulously asked.

"Would you say it's a palace, Brooke?"

I wasn't sure how to respond.

"I would!" he elatedly answered his own question. "It may be a small one, but I think it's a palace. It was modeled after Versailles."

"Yes," I said, "'The Little Palace'."

"Someone once told me that what makes a house a mansion is the number of bathrooms," he said. "That a house becomes a mansion when it has ten bathrooms. But I don't think bathrooms have anything to do with what makes for a mansion—do you?"

"I don't think so," I had to agree. "In any case, I'm sure you have ten."

"Though I suspect it's a palace rather than a mansion. I don't believe bathrooms have much to do with palaces, either. Do you?"

I concurred.

"So—what do you think?"

"About what?"

"Do you think it's a palace?"

"Tonight," I said, with unqualified conviction, "I'd have to say it's a palace."

As if his worst fear had been put to rest, he gazed across the ballroom. Then, leading me to an open terrace door, he looked out to the sea. "How do you like my boat?" he asked.

Across the balustrade, and down the lawn, rocked a pair of wooden masts. Perfectly restored, I already knew they must have hailed from the 1940s. I didn't need to be a freelance writer for Wooden Boat Magazine to know my eyes were about to fall onto the deck of a Concordia yawl.

"I didn't know you sailed!" I responded with surprise.

"To tell you the truth, I don't. In fact, it was you who inspired me to buy it!"

"Me?" I nervously asked.

"Wasn't that a print of a Concordia 39 unrolled on your desk?"

It was then that I was irrevocably convinced of Pickett's unexplained wealth. Educated as I was in the Eastern school of material understatement, I must confess an inborn suspicion of any ostentatious display; yet, it was hard to imagine a credible path from Pickett's working-class past to this consummate profile of affluence that had disappeared with the Depression. All I knew was, he had come to town with a thinning linen jacket on his back, and I had been left with my lost generation to make sense of his prophetic appearance.

Wielding a silver serving tray with an extraordinary flourish, our steward served the lord of the manor before attending to his guest. Perhaps embarrassed by the gaffe, Pickett raised his glass, granting me undeserved credit for his having come to Newport. The butler's tuxedo looked brand-spanking new, though his bowtie was slightly askew—giving me to note that he had missed a swathe of stubble on an otherwise clean-shaven chin.

"I thought gimlets would be appropriate!" Pickett sought my approval.

"I assume your man didn't come with the house."

Pickett almost cackled. "The truth is, I happened to meet Bernie downtown—West of Broadway! Or as he likes to be called, 'Bernard'. He told me he was once a Maître d'— though I'm not so sure about that. But Bernie needed a job, and I have to admit, it did seem providential!"

As Pickett looked out the Palladian window with his hands in the pockets of his suit—his handsome head tended in a longing way, and the light of the dying sun—I thought how, in the face of the undoubted jealousy that was sure to respond to his fortune, in that fleeting moment he looked as satisfied as any man could be. I wished it could be me, for all my so-called advantage in accomplishing what he had done; but bankrupt as I was by the prize of privilege, I knew it was another man's life. Rather than a life of ambition and greed to which his disadvantage might have led, he had uncannily fused wealth and innocence into a single mystifying whole.

Turning and surveying the storied room in all its epic proportions, for the first time I noticed massive packing crates scattered across the ballroom floor. The names 'Sotheby's' and 'Christie's' distinguished their containers from several lesser auction houses, before my eyes were drawn to a familiar-looking radio perched on top of one of them.

"What are *these*?" I asked, going over and kicking one of the containers.

"Furniture!" he laughed.

"It looks like you buy at all the right places!" I said.

Pickett vaguely nodded.

I pointed at the radio. "I certainly recognize that box!"

"It goes wherever I go!" he said.

"I wish I still had mine."

Silence filled the room.

"People are going to be jealous," I finally said.

"Jealous of what?"

"I could be wrong," I said.

"Why would anyone be jealous?"

"Maybe not everyone," I recanted, regretting having raised the prospect.

"Who?" Pickett curiously asked.

"People who want what you have."

"Whatever I have," he said, looking puzzled, "being jealous won't help them get it."

Walking back down the winding drive, the gardens now quiet and the laborers gone, I thought of Pickett standing in that celebrated room as though he had found his place. It might as well have been a century ago, I thought, looking back through the gate. Yet, then had marked the dawn of an age when anything could be done—free flight, railroads, industry, and wealth beyond compare—and now we were standing on the far side of a sun that promised 'manifest destiny', and revealed that even an eternal west was destined to come to an end.

As the firstborn babies of the Baby Boom, we were the firstborn children of the bomb, and believing that our future had been mortgaged to naught, hope no longer meant a thing. Like spoiled adolescents who exploited every freedom except the freedom to hope, we had chosen to destroy rather than regret what we couldn't have. Hope was everything to the man of this house—as it wasn't for the rest of us—and having given up on what we couldn't possess, we were fated to lose it all.

A note was awaiting me on my door when I got back home. Scrawled across a sales card promoting one kind of tennis racket or another, was the cryptic message:

Meet me at the club

Noon tomorrow

Ted

In a corner of the bridge room at the back of the club, enveloped in a cloud of Cuban smoke, sat Ted with another man I made out to be Leonard Madison. Ted was having lunch and talking at Leonard, stabbing his fork for emphasis. When he saw me, he got up, calling out my name for most of the house to hear.

"Let's get down to it," he said, leering as I sat down. "We have to do something about the priest."

"Pickett?" I came back.

"So, you're still sold on the drug dealer," he said.

"I didn't know he was one."

"Where the hell else did he get the money?"

"Newspapers," I said.

Ted looked across at Leonard—as though he'd been awaiting the opportunity.

"I checked with a friend at Sotheby's," Leonard said. "Pickett paid cash for Rosecliff. I don't know many men in the country with that kind of liquidity."

"Cocaine!" Ted triumphantly pronounced, lancing his fork in my direction.

"I can't think of a more unlikely dealer than Pickett," I protested.

Ted bore down on me. "It's one thing to be fair, Brooke boy," he said. "It's another thing to be naïve."

"Ted has asked me to look into it," Leonard mellifluously crooned.

"What are you going to do?" I objected.

"Check with the Feds."

"For what?"

"Recent drug movements, counterfeiting, stock frauds, stolen Treasury Bills."

"Well, you can count me out," I said, getting up.

Ted vindictively smirked. "Who's there to count out, Brooke boy?" he said. "For Christ's sake, you're already in!"

It didn't take a prophet to predict that Ted would be the first to be consumed. Jealousy was a mark of our idols as much as a mark of our time, and we had been left with a moral vacuum as big as Ted Talbot's ego. If we praised ourselves for democratic ideals extolling the virtue of freedom, what we had missed was the need for a rule that was bigger than us all.

Gone was the vicarious power of kings, and the dreams that princes once fulfilled for everyone else, who stood at the gate and believed that it was enough. In their place was a class of malcontents, who no longer knew where they stood, and like the proverbial kid in the candy store, took everything they could. Whether princes or kings were ever 'just', I had my serious doubts—history is filled with mercenary monarchs and shameless families like mine.

But as I stood with Pickett in one of the greatest houses in America, it was as though it took so great a paradox to transcend so divided a time. In a polarized world between those who had too little and those who had too much, we had become a disingenuous class of democratic wanna-be's. Either by God or an adulterated Darwin, we were the ones to rule, and had succumbed to the instincts of the entrepreneurs, and duplicitous presidents.

From the time he moved in and for the rest of the spring, I never saw the front gates open. Pickett had become a scarce commodity in town. Except for his weekly liturgical performance and greeting at the church door, I had little more contact with the fabled priest than knowing that we lived in the same town.

I saw him only once outside of church, while driving through the skids of Newport. Though I couldn't have imagined him on the streets anywhere west of Broadway, seeing his French car parked at the curb, I knew it had to be Pickett. Alarmed that Ted might have been right—that however innocent Pickett appeared, it wouldn't be the first time I was taken—I watched him talking to a tall Black man in an iridescent trench coat, who was listening intently to what I surmised were very specific instructions.

Pickett's presence, however phantasmal, was felt up and down the Eastern Seaboard. Camera-bearing pedestrians touring the mansions could be seen at the great iron fence, taking endless pictures, and listening intently as a verbose guide waxed innuendo about the house and its new proprietor. Cars from distant places predictably slowed where the deep green lawn began, backing up traffic along the Avenue for a quarter of a mile.

Every night, the house was ablaze with yellow light, giving the impression that the most social of gentlemen resided there. But for the many times I passed by in the dark, I never saw a sign of life. Only once did I think I glimpsed Athena's car racing out the service entrance—but checked myself as one more dreamer caught up in the fantasy of the time.

And I was not alone. Some said he was the miraculous union of worldly wealth and priestly beneficence that God had always intended, while others, that he was a New York mobster who covered his winnings as a cleric. Yet most didn't seem to care how it came to be—for all that really mattered was the myth which had built this town was alive again.

It was the middle of August when I received the invitation. It came by courier in a parchment envelope, engraved with the following announcement:

John Pickett and Co.

Request the honor of your presence for dinner

Saturday, August thirtieth,

At 8 o'clock in the evening

Rosecliff

Newport, Rhode Island

That night at the club, I loudly alluded to Pickett several times in hopes of jarring loose some information about who else might be going. I finally named the event to someone I thought was sure to know. Unfortunately, it was Winthrop Delafield, whose quip—"Being rich may well leave one with the same problems as being poor; all the same, I'd rather be rich"—had earned him the role of Newport patriarch, but whose drunken enthusiasm often resulted in betraying one's confidence.

Before I could stop him, he was boisterously working the crowded dining room, spreading the news that the elusive master of Rosecliff would host his first guest. "How did Adams do it?" I heard him say, his red face looking over each time he said it. "For God's sake," he hissed, past a dramatically cupped hand, "it's the only reason I've been going to church!"

It was as though we were starved for the kind of fulfillment that Pickett had ushered in. Not the kind which comes by work or competition, but by the simple, ineluctable fact that it had been ordained. If it appeared that Pickett dwelt in that house by nothing he had done on his own, it must have been by a God who had smiled on him from the day he was born.

On the evening of the dinner, I parked my car outside the open gates—perhaps in order to prepare myself for whatever awaited me. An odd sign of life was the light in the gatehouse. As I passed by a window, I looked inside and saw the back of a tall young woman; viewing her profile, I could have sworn that it was Elizabeth Van Fleet.

The gardens were restored to their original grandeur, laid out in the dusk like a beautiful woman and laden with roses. Walking through the sweet August air, I thought back to my life as a wakening boy, and that unexpected gift called love. No one had warned us of what love would bring—when a harmless coo from our mothers' lips, or social habit of family and friends—and then one day it was all that would matter, as destiny shone in her eyes, and the rest of the world that denied our faith would never matter again.

I thought how it wasn't the young boys who were fools, forced to endure such dismissive remarks as, "It's only infatuation," and "He's only in love with love." For they were the ones who feared love's excess as too great a gift to receive, and spent the rest of their dying days content they would not have to live. We were the ones who knew about love as God had always intended—that in the promise of her fairest face; in the truth of her beckoning eyes; in the roses and riches and sweet August air, love was all that would matter.

Bernie greeted me at the door—this time cleanly shaven. I even managed to coax a smile out of him. As I followed him in, I realized that what I had taken as condescension was just his best effort at living up to his hypothesis of a butler.

With a sweeping gesture, he directed me across the ballroom to the terrace. Walking through that spectacular space, the shipping crates now gone, the twilit air brought rose-colored life to the gilded furnishings. What sounded at first like a string quartet, albeit in a lower register, drifted in from the terrace past the long, tuxedoed back of the master of the house.

"Brooke!" I heard a melodic voice trill into the ballroom. It was Athena, peering around Pickett's shoulder with mischievous amusement. Before I could step out onto the terrace, Bernie was at my side—proudly presenting me with a Scotch from his trusty silver tray.

Pickett rushed in, apologizing for having neglected me. He took the remaining drinks from the tray, handed one to Athena, then raised his glass to what he proclaimed, "This penultimate moment!" Glancing at my watch—wondering when the rest of the guests would arrive—Athena discerned my puzzlement and laughed. "It's just the three of us, Brooke!"

Implying I had known this all along inspired more laughter from Athena. She excitedly led us onto the terrace, whence the music was coming. Smiling at Athena, Pickett politely aimed his glass at 'the string trio'—regretting that the second violinist couldn't make it, due to 'a terrible cold'.

After a tray of smoked salmon, then caviar, had made their several rounds, I was led into the dining room, where a breathtaking table was set. On an expansive sideboard, a sculpture of ice, vaguely resembling Rosecliff, was gushing forth liters of champagne from four illuminated chimneys. Pickett took his place at the head of the table, with Athena across from me; and as we sat down, her inscrutable grin eclipsed the sheening sea.

"Do you remember when I said if I could live in any house in the world, it would be this one?"

Before I could reply, she turned to our host. "I hardly thought you'd buy it!"

"Is it too much?" he anxiously asked.

"Not for a prince!" she delighted.

He nervously smiled. "I wish I were."

With her eyes fixed on him, she said, "You are."

For all my suspicions concerning Pickett's wealth after seeing him West of Broadway, in that moment, every doubt I had about this priest departed on an evening breeze. Despite my family's moral proscriptions about what makes for an upstanding life—overlooking the less than upstanding fact that the Adams had traded in slaves—every high-handed judgment I was born to wage against the inferior world suddenly gave way to the fullness of love I feared would never come again. Even the concern that Pickett was a scoundrel, and Ted might be proven to be right, dissolved in the verdant air of August, and the splendor of that luminescent night.

Watching them gaze at one another, I realized what they had. It was an indomitable love of youth that I had lost a decade ago—a love of hope, a love of trust, even a love of love, which bound them together in a covenant that the world would never tolerate. It was a love uncorrupted by greed, ambition, the unquenchable thirst for fame, which for the rest of us had unconsciously become the singular reason for living.

Theirs was a love unqualified, in all its possibilities, from schoolgirls, to paper boys, to the summer wind that blew through these terrace doors now. It was a love that harkened back to a distant past of a garden and a lilac limb, whose intoxicating fragrance was too overwhelming ever to be forgotten. In the end, it was a fathomless gratitude for all they had been given—if not for the unspoken, preposterous belief that it had been ordained by God.

I understood then why I had left Paris. It was not the failure of a journalistic effort that finally brought me home. It was the failure of a privileged life—which lost its sense of privilege.

At a time when my peers deemed 'destiny' a laughably archaic notion, Paris had beckoned from across the Atlantic as my last chance at a city of light. For seven years, wandering the streets and avenues with unrequited love lodged in my throat, I sought the incarnation of my heaven-bound dreams and found the earthly failings of myself.

Love had passed me by, with every lovely face that passed me by, or smiled to race my longing heart; and I was left, seven years hence, knowing how deprived a man who'd never had to try his dreams could be.

This was the difference between Pickett and me. Pickett had a faith that whatever the odds, the dream was worth the bet. If he already knew he was bound to fail, he knew he had no choice but to try—because however impossible may have been the dream, not to try was no less than to die.

Indeed, he had no choice in his great and humble life except to long, and chase the longing where it went. And I had every choice in my poor and prideful life to be satisfied and content. So, as I was sitting in that glorious house, smaller than I had ever felt, I feared I'd glimpsed too late the unimagined fate that another man was greater than I.

In the middle of an excellent Baked Alaska, the monumental dining room fell silent. Tings of sterling silver on elegant bone China rang across the parquet floor. At first, I thought I'd missed a cue between them, cryptically glanced across the table—and then I realized that what I might have missed was something greater than us all.

"It's too much, isn't it?" Pickett sighed, with unexplained resignation.

Athena smiled at me. "It *is* a bit big."

"A bit," I had to confess.

"But now we have Elizabeth!" Athena announced.

"Elizabeth is living here?" I asked.

"In the gatehouse!" she said.

"What—is she doing?"

"Reliving the past!" she laughed.

"I could move," Pickett unexpectedly spoke up.

The dining room fell silent.

"If the house is too big, I could move," he insisted.

"The Bishop's House is for sale!"

"Your old house?" I asked.

"The Diocese is tired of maintaining it."

"Let's buy it!" Pickett said.

Athena gazed at him. "You would do that—wouldn't you, John Pickett?"

"Tomorrow!" Pickett answered.

Athena turned to me. "John Pickett was our paper boy there."

"Though sadly…" she rejoined, "I don't remember him. As much as I wish I did."

Pickett looked embarrassed. "Paper boys aren't easy to remember," he imparted.

"Do you remember Athena?"

Pickett's face was flushed. "Yes, I believe I do!"

Athena raised her glass. "From paper boy prince to lord of the manor—in a decade!"

"Let's buy the Bishop's House," Pickett persevered.

She wistfully gazed at him. "Wasn't it Wolfe who said, 'You can't go home again'?"

"It was," Pickett replied.

"You don't look convinced," she flirted with our host.

"I'm not sure that you ever leave," he said.

Soon after I departed, explaining I was tired. I'm not sure why, except that I somehow knew the party was over—that despite the undeniable fact that the momentum of these hurricane weeks had never been greater, there was something in the sweet air of August which gave me to know it was the consummate force of a turning season. And

I knew what would be left when the winds had died, and darkness drew nearer the boundary of day, was a lingering trail of lighted dreams, making their way down the great green lawn to a place where life was borne by memory.

Approaching the gates, Elizabeth was leaning in the light of the gatehouse doorway. Above the crickets and the distant sea, I heard her softly singing; and though I bade her a pleasant evening, she continued to sing as though no one was there. When she was done, she looked vaguely my way, and breathed, "Hello, Brooke."

"You sang that as a child," I said.

"I'm still a child," she said.

"I suppose there's some of that in each of us."

"No—" she impatiently came back.

If at Elizabeth's wedding every sign of youth was gone, on this summer night of warmth and stars, it was unmistakably back. She was as lovely as she had been as a child—her fine translucent features, her penetrating eyes, her resolutely dark and shining hair.

"You know better than that," she said.

"There's a little of that in me?"

"Because you remember," Elizabeth said, bearing down on me. Looking back at Rosecliff, shining in the night, she said, "because he remembers." She held me in her gaze for an inexorable moment. "He remembers it all.

"I knew him then," she said. "I knew him in that time. We used to talk…at the gate."

"Did he ever tell you—how he felt about Athena?"

"He didn't have to tell."

"He's a good man," I said.

"He's better than that. He's a man who remembers the past."

"That was a long time ago," I lamented.

"Not as long as you think.

"Time is an illusion," Elizabeth said. "Only the truth lasts forever."

"Goodbye, Elizabeth," I said at last. But she was already singing.

When I got home, the phone was ringing. It was the gang in New York, inviting me down 'for Sunday brunch and a new proposal'. As it felt like an opportune time to leave Newport, I got up to catch the first train; but before I could close my overnight case, there was a knock on the door.

It was Pickett. He was still wearing his elegant tuxedo—though wilted in the sad way of children's costumes at the end of Halloween night.

"You left early," he said.

"Yes," I said. "I was ready for bed."

"It wasn't the party?"

"Oh, no," I replied. "It was a wonderful party."

He looked relieved. "It wasn't—" he said, and hesitated.

"Too much?"

"Yes," he said.

"No," I reassured him. "It was a wonderful party."

I thought I had him roundly convinced when he came back with a last interrogation. "It wasn't—the chimneys?"

"The chimneys—" I repeated.

"On the ice palace," he said. "To be honest, that was Bernie's idea. I suddenly feared in the middle of dinner that champagne flowing from lighted chimneys may have been too much."

"No," I said. "It wasn't too much."

"I didn't have the heart to tell him."

"If Rosecliff had chimneys," I cast my vote, "it would have been exactly right."

"It wasn't—that you disapproved," he persisted.

With another man, I might have grown impatient by this time, but with Pickett, it was different. "Disapproved of what?"

"Of Athena—and me. Of course, we're not living together."

I probably nodded.

"It's just the way—the way it was meant to be."

I wondered how long it had been since I believed in a 'way it was meant to be'. Perhaps it was having lost parents too young that made me doubt there was such a thing. Yet in that moment I couldn't help thinking it was lost somewhere along the garden wall—where innocence and love, where hope and destiny, were fleetingly one and the same—protecting fearless dreamers from a spineless generation of cynics and hardhearted bastards who had come to believe that nice guys finished last, and hope endured at too great a cost.

"Brooke, did you ever have a dream that came back?"

"A recurring dream?" I asked.

"That's it—yes! A recurring dream," he repeated with satisfaction.

"I have," he reflected. "A dream that came back—again, and again, and again. Each time it was different." He looked perplexed. "But somehow it was always the same.

"Her age was never the same," he said. "But the place was always the same. A lovely place—surrounded by a lovely garden wall. A lovely, peaceful place…yet always full of excitement, and beauty, and grace.

"To this day I can smell it, the sweet scent of decay…though not of something that was dying. It was the scent of earth and roots, of burgeoning growth, the intoxicating scent of life.

"The scent of possibility, the scent of innocence, the scent of unspeakable romance…which gave you to know that no matter how disappointing life could be…no matter how lousy a hand you were dealt, for nothing you had done on your own…there would always be a promised land, just around a corner. There would always be a destined garden…waiting for you to come in.

"The dream…was always the same," he mused. "I was always young—and without much money. I must have been a paper boy—though I don't remember my bag. But somehow, I could never get past the stone gate, as open as it always seemed. All I can remember is, no matter how I tried, I could never get in."

"The Bishop's Garden," I said at last.

Pickett looked up—almost startled.

"And it was Athena."

It was then he sighed, as though he had been found out. "I could never see her face. Though the dreams were just of her, and each time I awoke I would whisper her name a thousand times, I could never see her face—because it was always receding into the garden.

"And then a year ago, when I saw her in the pew—" he cleared the catch in his throat. "I knew that however disappointing life could be, there was a way—I could get in."

Listening to this unaccountable priest, I remember feeling confounded: by who Pickett was, by whence he had come, and by how he had been able to survive. He seemed oblivious to the world in which we lived, if not to what adulthood meant. It was as though he'd never learned the rules of the game—of bars, and angling, and single-night sex—and found a life greater than the rest of us knew, or ever could have imagined.

As he spoke, he brought back every boyhood innocence that I had somehow forgotten—when the world was a stage on which to realize whatever stirred the yearning heart. I tried to remember what it was that must have distracted me. It was as though I had unwittingly come to assume that the loss was just a casualty on the inevitable road from ignorance to becoming a certified adult.

I realized it wasn't the stage that had failed. It was the players who had failed, and become an audience that no longer believed in itself. Perhaps our undoing was the intervening years, when we no longer saw what Pickett saw—that only by remembering whence we had come would we ever make our mark—and so we set about creating a future that felt worthy of forsaking the past, in a frenzy of success that glorified the war rather than facing our regret.

"Brooke, have you had a recurring dream?"

"Yes," I had to confess.

"And?"

I shook my head.

"Where is she?" Pickett asked.

"I'm not sure. Paris, I think."

"So, what are you waiting for?" he pressed.

"Sometimes dreams pass away."

He looked at me—as though I should have known better. "Not as long as there's tomorrow."

The train to New York was almost empty. I was about to sit down when I glimpsed a familiar-looking head further up in the car. It was Tapley, peering nonchalantly out the window from her first-class seat.

I considered a retreat, but before I could take cover, she happened to glance up. Unavoidably caught, I ventured forth. "What have you been up to?"

She acknowledged me without the faintest look of surprise. It appeared she had gained some weight. "I'm selling out, Brooke. You know me. I'm always selling out."

"I thought Ted was out of town," I said, accepting the offer to join her.

"I wouldn't know," she answered. "I'm in New York now, Brooke. I'm just here to sell my condo."

Before I could respond, she condescended, "But I see *you're* still here."

"Most of the time."

"Though the tales of Father Pickett have found their way to Manhattan."

She eyed me—brazenly. "Well, is it true?"

"Is what true?" I resisted.

"That he paid five million cash for Rosecliff," she said.

"I believe that's the rumor."

"And how—is it rumored—did he get it?" she inquired.

"I wouldn't know," I countered.

"I heard it was drugs."

"I heard it was newspapers."

"Come, Brooke—you don't believe that."

"I believe in Pickett."

"I believe in the truth."

"Dreams can be true," I said.

"Dreams are never true," she summarily replied.

"Dreams are all we have," I said.

Tapley cocked her head—as if in disbelief. "This doesn't sound like the Brooke Adams I once knew," she said. Something was troubling her. "Dreams are for those who can't have what they want. I believe in having what I want."

"And what do you want?"

"Money!" she laughed. "The moment—and tennis champions!"

I didn't take the bait.

She stared at me. "Two out of three ain't bad."

"Don't tell me you lost your money," I said.

"Very funny. I lost my tennis balls."

Reaching for her bag on the compartment floor, she drew out a gold cigarette case.

"I'm sorry," I said.

She lit a cigarette, producing a great cloud of smoke. "It doesn't matter," she exhaled, with laden eyes. "He's over the hill, anyway."

"What happened to eternal love?"

"A thing of the past," she hissed.

"What's wrong with the past?"

"Nothing," she said. "Except that it's irrelevant."

We got off the train at Grand Central Station and parted beneath the clock. She held out her hand. "Good luck, Brooke Adams! Good luck with recovering your past!"

"Thank you," I said. "And good luck with your future."

"Remember? I only have the moment."

"One woman's moment becomes her past."

She laughed, "You sound like Pickett!"

"I'll take that as a compliment," I said.

She looked me in the eye. "Please—do."

The weekend in New York was laced with the sobering realization that, denials notwithstanding, we were all turning the corner into the comfort of our thirties. It came not only from my compulsive need to survey my cohorts' growing girths, or the sense I had in all of them that it was time to give over our freshman hopes to the disappointing ways of the world. It was the recognition that staying young would not be won by having been born that way.

I felt a sinking disappointment as I forced myself to listen to the new proposal—an 'alternative entrepreneurial journal for young urban professionals'. It was as though I was in a room full of strangers who pretended that they knew me, or refused to admit to the evident fact that I had become an outsider. Following our host's opening pitch, I withdrew into disillusionment, trying to imagine another way back to my longest, firstborn dreams.

Returning on the train, there was no longer a question about having to leave Newport. If I wondered whether it had gotten too small, I was sure that my time had grown short. So, as I watched that deep green spit of land rise from the water before me, I resolved to make a definitive move and be gone by September's end.

Chapter 9

At first, I didn't recognize Ted's voice on the phone. He had to see me 'immediately', he barked like a dog chained to a fence; and driving to the Point, I wondered if it had anything to do with reality. When I got to the door, he was standing behind it—his face concentrated in a scowl.

"Follow me," he said, leading me back through the hall to his study. Leonard was standing in the middle of the room—puffing a cigar and peering at one of Ted's magazines on the desk. Seeing me, he waved and came purposefully over like a man who had a role to play.

"Leonard's uncovered the scam," Ted said, gritting his teeth in a grin.

"What scam?" I came back.

He gloatingly smirked—clearly relishing the information. "Pickett's scam," he triumphantly imparted. "Go ahead—tell him, Leonard!"

"Last Sunday, I was sitting in a pew, waiting for the service to begin, when it suddenly struck me that Pickett's fortune might have something to do with the church. So, on my way out, I told the treasurer that I could count the collection, and since I had keys from my treasurer days, would close up the building myself."

Ted was hanging on Leonard's every word, virtually wheezing with delight. I desperately wanted to leave just then, but stayed on the instinct that no matter where I went, the dye had already been cast.

"With the church all my own," Leonard rolled on, "I went straight to the bell tower ledger. When I found it, I expected to see all the money, or, as likely, nothing at all. But not only was there half a million," he chortled, "there was that and ten million more!"

Ted's face took on a menacing grimace, as if he were about to devour the next unsuspecting visitor who came into the room. "That was my goddam money!" he ranted. "That was my goddam money!"

From what I was able to piece together, Leonard cashed in a favor with a Newport judge and secured an audit on Pickett's bank account—which was opened with half a million. When the account was 'zeroed out', Leonard deduced the money had gone into the market, and from there researched every big-moving issue over the past six months. Since there was only a handful of stocks that had seen a fifty-fold return, it was simply a matter of obtaining a warrant to discover their largest holders.

"And the first issue I looked at," Leonard regaled, "was the gold stock, Treasure Valley! And what do you know, Pickett once held half a million shares!"

Leonard couldn't recall if he had ever mentioned the stock in Pickett's presence, and I refused to give him the satisfaction that he had.

"From penny stock to forty bucks a share!" Leonard baited his client. He looked at me. "If Ted had taken my advice, that would have been *his* twenty million."

"It *is* my twenty million!" Ted decried. "Or at least half of it!"

Leonard turned to me. "Not to rub it in, but Pickett sold right at the top." He shook his head. "I have to admit, I couldn't have done it any better."

Ted looked like a tick that was about to pop.

"What's it to you?" I chided him. "Or to the church, for that matter! All Pickett did was double the take—the church is ten million to the good!"

Ted blew his stack. "It's my goddam money! Half that money is mine! And goddam it—" he vowed, "I'm gonna get it back! The church can have the rest!"

"That's your sordid business," I disgustedly replied. "Yours—and the bloody church's."

"And I'll tell you something else! That newspaper—'Spare Change'? It's history! I'm ending it tomorrow!"

"What newspaper?" I said.

"Pickett's!" Ted bellowed. "So, do you trust him now? He started a goddam newspaper downtown—filled with stories written by the homeless! Can you fucking believe it—a newspaper written by the lazy about how to be lazy?"

"Lazy?" I retorted.

"Lazy!" he demanded.

"Maybe they're unlucky," I said.

"They're lazy!" he rebutted.

"Some of the laziest people I know are rich."

"Who are you talking about?" he lashed out.

It was clear I had struck a nerve.

As though the weight of my past had been lifted from my shoulders, I said, "I'm talking about me."

Leaving his office, I turned in the doorway. "So, what are you going to do?"

"Nothing, Brooke, boy! It's out of our hands!"

"What does that mean?" I shot back.

"When Leonard got the warrant, the Feds had to come in!"

"And what are *they* going to do?"

Ted leered at me, savoring the moment. "Arrest the swindler," he said.

It was this last pronouncement which brought to the stage the dreaded climax of a season of acts. However I wanted to hold at bay the seemingly inevitable, with my thumb in the dike, I knew the sea was about to come crashing in. Now that it was a federal case, there was nothing I could do—what was lurking in the wings of this unfolding drama was finally about to happen.

"They haven't taken him yet?"

"He's up in Massachusetts. Burying an uncle or something."

When I got home, Athena was sitting on my stoop in all her beauty. Though she looked to be smiling, as I approached, it became an uncertain smile. As if anticipating disapproval, she called, "I need a witness!"

"When it comes to you, I'd vow for anything!"

"For giving up?" she implored.

Her lips began to quiver. "I'm leaving Ted," she said. Her eyes welled up with tears.

"Brooke, you don't have to be the one to sign."

Staring at the tear-soaked summons, I instantly felt sick. Though I should have felt relief for this woman I loved— who had always deserved so much more than the likes of

Ted Talbot could give her—overcome as I was by all that had happened, I couldn't help but sense that this was less an accident of love than the train wreck of a generation.

"I told you," I said, "when it comes to you, I'd vow for anything." I took her hand, and she dejectedly stood up from the old stone stoop. Throwing her arms around my neck, she sobbed into my shoulder. I held her there—for probably too long—before I let her go.

"How the hell did you end up with Ted?"

Her laughter let a spill of tears. "I don't know," she said, looking up. "I must have thought it was over."

"What was over?"

"That—kind of love."

"What kind?"

"The only kind," she said.

"Pickett's kind?" I asked.

"Yes," she grieved. "The never-ending kind."

Unexpectedly, she laughed.

"What is it?" I said.

She sobbed. "Pickett—is a virgin!"

I started. "A—what?"

"Pickett is a virgin!"

"I didn't know—"

"There was—such a thing?"

With a devastated heave, she laughed again, then shuddered. "Neither did I!"

As difficult as it was to imagine any grown man as a virgin—in a time when virginity was aberrant behavior to be cured by psychotherapy—as I held her in my arms, I couldn't help but feel, for all the pleasures of sowing our oats, that for a man like Pickett, such passing satisfactions would have come at too great a cost.

"What's—worse," she succumbed to a last torrent of tears, "I'm afraid—he will always be!"

"Nor did I know—"

"*That* was possible?" she laughed—and sobbed again. "It—isn't!"

"When did it end?" I asked at last.

She knew what I was asking. "When we decided we were smarter than love."

"Were we—smarter than love?"

"That's the wrong question."

"What's the right question?"

"Did we love enough," she said.

"Did we love enough?"

She looked me in the eye. "We can never love enough."

"So, Pickett never loved enough?"

She ironically smiled—as though she had been caught. "Pickett always knew he never loved enough. Which is why he always loved enough."

With that, I took the summons. "I'll sign," I said. "I'll sign in the interest of love."

It was a steamy afternoon, and I spent the hours until evening lazing about the shaded corners of the house, resting my bare feet on every cool-looking piece of furniture I could find, and mourning the passing of those college days when such choices were as tough as life got. There was a warm wind high up in the trees, defying the heat with its refreshing sound, and through the screens came the melancholic sweetness of times now gone. If the elders of my childhood would always believe that I was eight years old, I knew I would always be twenty.

For this is the year in every man's life—after the ardor of adolescence is over and before the labor of adulthood—when the world stands before him in its elegant green grandeur, to realize his every freedom. Yet thanks to the circumstances of my life, I was left with too little to do, except to serve a lifetime sentence for having achieved nothing on my own. As anxious as I was about Pickett's plight, and the certain prison in his future, the irony was, of the two of us, he was the one who was free.

At 6 o'clock, I was standing in my summer kitchen, staring at bare cupboards, and wondering if I stood there long enough, would the makings of dinner appear. I should have noticed in these passing weeks that there was less and less food in the house, and unconscious as it was, that I was already preparing for my departure. I finally relented, and called the club to say that I was coming.

As I entered, several gazes followed me to the Maître d' stand. I asked to sit out on the veranda, where I anticipated a dearth of hail and hearty diners this late in the season. Indeed, as I sat down, there was only a party of three on the other end.

One of them was Ted, conversing intently at a table with two other men. Next to him sat Leonard, and in civilian attire, the third was the Bishop of Rhode Island. I ordered a drink and a light dinner, and by the time the drink came, I sensed that Ted already knew I was there.

He chose the moment of my dinner's arrival to come over and confront me. "I hardly had you for a traitor!" he carped, expanding his shoulders as he came.

I barely looked up.

"Of anyone, Brooke, I didn't think you'd be the one to sign."

"I didn't know witnesses could be indicted."

"Christ, Brooke!" he said, sitting down. "You might as well have put the last nail in our coffin!"

"It's what you wanted all along."

"Goddam it—how many times do I have to say it!"

I didn't respect the question.

"I love Athena!" he obsequiously pleaded. "And I swear to God, I always will!"

"You should have told Athena that."

"I told her!" he griped. "But for some reason, she won't believe me!"

"It might have had something to do with Tapley."

"Christ, Tapley didn't mean a goddam thing."

"It did to Athena."

"You think I'm a bastard, don't you, Brooke?" he said.

I ignored the self-pity.

"For Christ's sake, Brooke, I thought I was your friend."

"Pickett is my friend."

"And…he may go free."

He could see he had my attention.

"We worked it out," he nobly reported. "The church is dropping the charges."

"In exchange for what?"

"What does that mean?"

"No strings attached?" I asked.

"Not to Pickett!"

"To whom?" I fired back.

Uneasily, he looked away.

"To Athena," I said.

He went on the offensive. "Goddam it! Athena is my wife!"

"The strings are attached to Athena," I said.

"She just has to stay with me."

"You've got to be kidding. That's what you worked out with the bloody bishop?"

"That and Rosecliff," he brashly announced.

"That—and Rosecliff?" I said.

"The church is selling the house and we're splitting the proceeds."

"You're taking back your donation?"

"That, and what it made for me."

"Half—the ten million?" I gasped.

"Twenty," Ted freely imparted. "Pickett came out with twenty."

In that moment, he had the eyes of a dragon. I realized then it wasn't just the money; it was the need to vanquish the opponent. As fatefully as Pickett had gotten in Ted's way, the truth was, it wasn't only Ted—it was the rest of us, who would rather die the winner than live a life worth losing.

"Shame on us," I finally said.

"Then shame on the church!" Ted said. "Anyway, what the hell does it matter? The bishop's about to defrock him!"

I didn't sleep that night. By 1 o'clock, I suspected I was going to be out on the porch till morning. An off-shore breeze rattled the late September trees, and at two I decided to get up and go out in search of a fallen gust.

Ironic as it seemed, as I left the house, I felt unutterably homeless. I realized then that there must be a difference between being houseless and homeless, because as grateful as I was to have a roof above my head, none of it made sense anymore. Having repressed my longing for a home since my parents' death at three years old, the truth that had come to the Adams' front door was that I no longer had one.

I wondered if this was what it meant to be a man without a country. If so, it wasn't just a homeland I had lost; it was a family legacy, which for three hundred years was inseparable from its 'manifest destiny'. It was as though our time had finally run out in a land that had never been ours—where we had fallen prey to the illusion of possession that our elders saw for what it was—and now we were facing the telltale signs of the beginning of an end, on a desecrated landscape of ambition and greed where we no longer saw the sea.

Bellevue Avenue was moonlit and empty, and wandering up the silver road in pursuit of a last enchantment, I relished this opportunity to have it as my own. I laid claim as I went to every empty mansion that lurked in the darkness of that night, wishing these dreams now gone to museums could miraculously come back. But I knew they would not—even in the face of that rising palace ahead—holding at bay what I already knew stood as an inevitable end.

The house was cast in darkness. Hovering at the crest of the hill like a ship anchored in the night, Rosecliff was awash in a sea of stars as though it had always been. However we had tried to extinguish its glory by these late, vainglorious days, I couldn't help believing in an order of perfection that was bound to be with us forever.

My eyes ran along the fence to the gate when I was startled by a ghostly presence—a darkling shadow, eerily cast at the foot of the shimmering drive. As I approached, I discerned a tall, lean figure in a double-breasted suit, looking away down the Avenue as if it were expecting someone. His hair was combed against the temples and shone in the light of the moon; and a worn leather suitcase sat at his feet, perched on the glistening drive.

"Pickett?" I called.

He turned with a start. "Brooke!" Pickett called back.

Arriving on the drive, I shook his hand. "It's good to see you," I said.

He nodded and smiled.

"How are you?" I asked.

"Tomorrow is sure to be better!"

"I heard you had a funeral."

"The last I'll ever do!"

"I'm sorry."

"Thank you, Brooke," he said.

"An uncle?" I inquired.

"Yes," he said. "An uncle, and a very old friend."

"Did you have quite a crowd?"

"Oh, no!" Pickett laughed. "I was all Gordon had left."

"When I said I was sorry—" I tried to clarify, "I meant—sorry about it all."

"About what?" Pickett asked.

"About—everything," I said.

"But there's nothing to be sorry about!"

I swallowed hard.

"I have all I ever wanted—largely thanks to you!"

"Thanks to me?"

He stared with puzzlement. "Brooke, you brought me back to Athena!"

If it were possible to bottle Pickett's gratitude, I would have taken a case. For his preposterous hopes, which in any other man would have been dashed on the rocks of disappointment—his unreachable dreams, so near they must have brushed the heel of his outstretched hand—as he felt them slipping through his trembling fingers, and the towering gates of Rosecliff, they had somehow rendered not disillusionment, but untold gratitude. This was the difference between Pickett and me: I, who had been given everything the world was purported to offer, was as empty a man as Pickett was replete with the riches we both had sought.

"Is there anything I can do?" I asked.

"Thanks, Brooke. There's really nothing."

"What are you going to do?" I inquired.

"Actually—I'm not sure. I'm waiting for Athena."

"When—is she coming?"

"She should have been here by now."

Together we gazed down the Avenue.

"She must be deciding. I'm quite sure that she'll come. It's only a matter of time."

"How long will you wait?"

"The night," he replied. "There isn't much of it left!"

"What—if you get caught?"

"I suspect I'll go to prison."

"Ted said you can go free if—"

"Brooke," Pickett said. "Without Athena, I will never be free."

He looked at his watch, then down the Avenue again. "I'm quite sure that she'll come," he said at last. "One way or the other, she'll come."

"Where will you live—one way or the other?"

"I'm not sure. It really doesn't matter."

"I could find you a—"

"Thanks, Brooke," Pickett said. "But it doesn't matter at all."

Arriving back home, the damp September air curdled with the first signs of dawn. The moment that my head hit the pillow, I was already plunged into a restless sleep. When I started awake to an unsettled gut, change was in the air; getting up, I went to the kitchen to discover it was already noon.

With coffee in hand, I collected the mail—which contained a letter from Paris. I'd been recommended to an editor at the International Tribune who, unbeknownst to me, was given several features I wrote for "An American in Paris." Before I could restrain myself, I put in a call to the editor in question; and by the time I returned the phone to the cradle, I was an expatriate again.

As auspicious a change as this marked in my life, I was seized by inexplicable guilt. Taking in the Rosa rugosa, sweetly blown in from the sea, I whiled away the afternoon, pondering all that had happened. Haunted by what felt like an unsettling dream, weaving in and out of consciousness, by 5 o'clock I had no choice but to brave the truth a final time.

A 'Sotheby's International' sign was planted on the front lawn. Athena's car was parked at the door, though

Ted's was nowhere to be seen. Ringing twice, I opened the screen and entered the house, unannounced.

I was already hoping they wouldn't be at home when I heard a mournful cry. Racing through the entry to the back of the house, there in the solarium was a lithe, young woman, limply draped like a towel over a loveseat arm. When I cleared my throat, she wildly looked up through a tangled fall of hair; and before she could rake it behind an ear, I thought it was Elizabeth.

She made no effort to get up. Staring at me with dark, empty eyes, I realized it was Athena. As trusted a confidante as I had been from that fateful day in Ashfield, I knew that none of my sibling banter would ever make her happy again.

"It's Pickett, isn't it?" I said at last.

"It will always be Pickett."

I tried to coax a smile. "It isn't Ted?"

"It has to be Ted," she said.

"Why can't you leave?"

"I can never leave."

"Pickett was waiting," I said.

"I—know," she balanced a wellspring of tears. "But better—than waiting in prison."

Through the sunroom windows behind her head, I saw Ted down on the tennis court—ambling about and occasionally leaning down to snatch up a weed. Knowing his uncanny intuition, I suspected that he knew I was there. As I beheld Athena's lovely face in its pale and tearful exhaustion, her resplendent beauty in the midst of the wreckage would be with me until I died.

"Goodbye, Brooke," she said, as though she knew it was time.

"Goodbye, Athena," I said.

"Say goodbye to him—will you?" she breathed. "Say goodbye—for us all."

As well as I knew it was the closing act, like a proverbial moth to the flame, I was inexorably drawn to the incendiary source I sensed was waiting to consume me. Instead of continuing on to my car, I started down the lawn toward the sea. Stopping at a great rhododendron by the house before venturing out into the open, there he was, kneeling on the court like an acolyte at the altar.

It was as though I had been the unnamed accomplice who had never gotten caught. I was the consummate confidence man who had so perfected his craft that, thanks to his righteous pleas and admonitions, had successfully lived beyond suspicion. It was not for anything I had done that made me feel like I'd gotten caught; it was for everything I had failed to do to stem this self-destructive tide.

"The tennis season's over!" I called.

Ted cavalierly looked up. "No one gives a damn about tennis anymore."

"Guilty as charged," I said.

"The game went out with Forest Hills," he ignored the remark.

"Like wooden boats," I said.

He laughed. "Like wooden boats!"

"Did you sell Pickett's?" I asked.

He yanked out a weed. "The bow!" he barked. "The bishop got the stern."

"And a beautiful boat sank to the bottom."

"I'll get my money," he said.

"So, that's enough?" I said.

"It's always enough."

"And a beautiful boat is gone."

"That's the way it is."

"It didn't have to be."

His puny eyes fixed on me. "You don't like me, do you, Brooke?"

"I don't like our time."

"I am our time," he said.

"Then I don't like you, Ted."

"Who *do* you like?"

"A man who knows to let a woman go."

"And let a loser win?"

"Otherwise, all of us are losers," I said.

"Speak for yourself," he said.

"I just did," I said. "I spoke for both of us."

"Go to hell," he said.

I held him there a moment, before I finally said, "We're already there."

I knew that no matter how I pleaded my case, no matter how convincing I might be—no matter how I tried to inspire the slightest empathy in a guy like Ted—nothing would redeem a hubris so embedded in a whole generation, that none of us could even remember what it was that we forgot. Liberals, conservatives, lawyers, politicians, businessmen, and tennis players, we were in it together, throwing philanthropic bones at the system just to keep it going. The mayhem that would follow, as my uncle would have said, was 'as sure as God made little green apples', giving me to fear our only difference from Ted was that the rest of us didn't play tennis.

When I got back to my car, dusk was settling in the tops of the great oak trees. I turned around to see a blood-red sun, falling immensely to the sea. But as I got in, Elizabeth was standing at the foot of the greatest tree—wearing a virgin-white cotton dress, and staring intently at me.

"Are you going?" she impassively said.

"Going where?" I asked.

"To Rosecliff," Elizabeth stoically replied. "It may be your last chance to see him."

She looked lovely—perhaps even more lovely than I had ever seen Athena—and I wondered how a young girl's life that was so right could ever turn out so wrong. "He needed to retrieve some things," she said. "The police brought him here to get permission."

As I started the car, she came forward from the tree and filled my window with her countenance. "They all thought I was crazy," she calmly said—with disconcerting reason. "Even Athena thought I was crazy. But now she knows that I wasn't."

The winding pebble drive was pink with petals, falling from the gardens in the cold, and the glazed terra cotta continued to glow in the dying of the setting sun. Two police cars were parked along the front, and a cop was stationed at the door. Assessing me with military suspicion, I told him that I knew Ted; and he immediately smiled and stepped aside, allowing me to go in.

Traversing the gleaming foyer floor to the edge of the ballroom, I stood in the entry to remember one last time my evening with the two of them. Walking to the middle, I faced the bank of windows opened to the setting sun, filling the room with a lingering breeze of roses blown in from the sea. The church had made fast work of the house, leaving a Steinway in the corner, and outdoor furniture against the balustrade in a nest of windblown leaves.

"Brooke!" came a voice—and then crisp, staccato steps resounding across the ballroom floor.

I turned to see him striding through the infinite space in his elegant double-breasted suit; and his hair, catching the last of the light, was combed as it was the night before. Deliberately clutching the familiar yearbook and picture frame against his chest, the memorable white plastic radio was tucked under the other arm. As he approached, I couldn't help being surprised that he managed to be smiling—as though it was his to offer his guest a final consolation.

"I'm sorry," I preempted him.

"Thank you, Brooke," he said. "You know she didn't come."

"She wanted to," I said.

"It's all that matters—in the end."

"If you need any money," I made my final plea.

"No, Brooke. Thanks," he said.

"What are you going to do?" I asked.

"I'm not really sure," he said.

"Do you still have the proceeds from the house in Six Bridges?"

"Oh, no, that went to Gordon."

"Your uncle?" I asked.

"Yes!" he laughed. "He went through it all before he died!"

His seeming nonchalance gave me to fear for his impending financial future. "Money isn't a problem," I insisted. "You wouldn't have to pay me back."

"Thank you, Brooke. But it isn't the money. It was never the money."

Chapter 10

In a matter of days, the Talbots were gone and their house was said to be sold, and from what I was able to glean at the club, I was the last to see Pickett. With every reason to stay now gone, save the indulgence of regret, my bags were packed, the house closed up, and the caretaker, aware of my leaving. My last weekend in town, I rose with the sun and sat out in the garden, pondering what seemed likc an eternity since the day I met Pickett.

I thought how we lived in a jealous time, and that if it were allowed to go on too long, it was probably going to kill us. Unlike the years before Indochina—when however far from the monarchy we believed we had come, there remained a faint, vestigial remembrance of a right and just order of things—now we suffered the anarchy of blind ambition and greed, where heaven-bound hopes became earthward strokes to keep the next man down. Something happened to douse our hopes, our dreams of Camelot, which made the promise of God and King a remnant of the past.

Something happened that took these hopes from everyone I knew, except the few who dared to believe such dreams could only come true. Perhaps it was only for lack of courage that we cowered from a greater life, which

Pickett had known for one shining moment before the curtain came down. For in the end, it was people like Ted who were finally the cowards—running a suicidal race we all believed we could win.

Like the preacher's kid who never saw his father, we were orphans of the '80s, left to travel from pillar to post with no moral compass but money. The church was in bed with the rest of us, hoisted on its own petard, in hopes of winning some vicarious success that would make it a part of the club. But the only one in charge was Pavlov's dog—fame, acclaim, some reach for redemption that was doomed from the very start—leaving us to sift through ashes of success amid a burgeoning funeral pyre of yesterday's headlines, in search of something we couldn't remember we had lost.

The day before I left, a soft September rain swept in from the shore, and I got in my car in hopes of sating a final curiosity. The last lingering tourists had left with the sun, and memories of another summer, and the end of the season appeared to have silently shuttered the houses on its own. The lovely desolation of the rain-soaked wild that rolled along the sound, abruptly gave way to the urban desolation that redlined West of Broadway.

Getting out of my car, the buffeting wind slammed the driver's door shut. As I started down the walk, a sheet of rain almost swept me into the bay. With my head into the wind, and my eyes bearing down on sodden litter skidding on the walk, I happened to look up to a front page of 'Spare Change', randomly plastered to a lamppost.

Further down the street, through the pelting rain, there he was on the corner—tall and erect like a regal bowsprit, just as I remembered him. Drenched as it was, I nonetheless recognized the iridescent trench coat. With one foot planted on a newspaper stack, he looked to be lost in thought.

If not for what felt like a magnetic field, I would have passed on the far side of the street. Yet something kept me west of Broadway. As I neared, I feared that he might sense this was more than happenstance—but overcoming my trepidation, I launched the fortuitous exchange.

"Is that 'Spare Change'?" I glanced at the stack.

He grinned. "It will be if you buy one!"

I dug into my pocket.

"Though I have to admit, the news is gittin' pretty old."

"News is always getting old," I said, handing him a dollar.

"Ain't that the truth?"

"When did you stop publishing the paper?" I asked.

He peered at me—guardedly. "When Father Pickett got arrested.

"Did you know him?" he asked.

I hesitated. "Yes," I said at last.

"Was he a friend of yours?"

"Yes," I said. "Pickett will always be my friend."

His eyes softened—as though he knew I could be trusted. "Shame on them," he said.

A cold sheet of rain luffed up from the bay, sending a chill into my frame. Looking back in the direction whence I came, I said, "Shame on us all."

"Excuse me?" he enacted a comedic double-take.

"I said, shame on us all."

Caught between a world I no longer wanted and one to which I didn't belong, I realized I had more in common with this stranger than with any of my erstwhile friends. It was as though the world where I grew up had become an alien land, and with the rest of them, I had been left without a legacy, a country, or a home. As absurd as it would have seemed to my chums, he was already beyond us—seeing through the illusions of success, to glimpse an eternal sea.

Looking up and down the empty block, he mischievously grinned at me. "Don't mean no disrespect," he said, "but you white guys worra' too much about money."

I howled: "You don't?"

His pensive eyes smiled. "I got nothin' to worra' about."

In that moment, my gut turned inside out—from hilarity to disgrace.

"What about you?" he curiously asked.

"I've got too much to worry about."

He winced. "What's your name?"

"Brooke," I said.

"My name's Willie," he said.

He reached out his hand with a gentleness that defied his iron fist.

"It must be disappointing," I said. "The end of 'Spare Change', I mean."

Considering the thought, he generously smiled. "Life is full of disappointments."

If ever I had met a man who shouldn't have been able to afford generosity, it was one who was left in the pouring rain by another man who had too much. To this day I fail the paradox which shone in his beneficent eyes—that generosity comes by way of knowing in the end, it's all we have. As for Ted, as for me, as for all of us who feared we would never be enough, we hid behind our money and our sad accomplishments, and missed the greater life we could have lived.

"I don't know how you can be generous," I said.

"Me, or my people?" he asked.

"Both," I said.

His eyes fixed on me, as though he knew something that I didn't. "I suppose when you're on the end we're on," he said, "you know how bad it is not to be."

"Bad for you?"

"That's just the point. Bein' selfish is bad for everyone."

"I'm sorry," I said, nodding in the direction of Bellevue Avenue.

"For what?" he asked.

"The selfishness," I said.

"Though it didn't seem to work for you!"

I tried to laugh.

"Don't be," he said. "Be generous, like our friend."

"I'll never forget him," I said at last.

"He's unforgettable! I'll give them that!"

"I hope he'll be remembered," I said.

He winked. "That's up to you and me."

With my cab scheduled to arrive at eight the next morning, I was up at the crack of dawn. It was as though the house and family homestead for more than two hundred years, could no longer host the bankrupt life I had allowed myself to live. Or maybe it knew that there comes a time for the master to be set free, to know what it means not to have a home in order to find one again.

I wondered if this was what Pickett had sought as a fledgling paperboy prince—some ordained destination that felt like home in a world where he didn't belong. And I wondered if he'd glimpsed it in the bishop's garden, and Athena's perfect face: some shining constellation of an accident of stars by which to reconstruct a broken world. I even wondered if this was the dream he had chased by his singular obsession with Athena, from outlier in college to lord of one of the grandest houses in the land, gleaning the past for a prophetic vision that might lead him from his desolate Six Bridges to a place that embodied a consummate love he came to understand as God.

Whether it was Rosecliff or West of Broadway, it didn't seem to matter to him. However fantastical may have been the dream, it was only the dream that mattered. What bound together Pickett's contradictions was the paradox of life itself—that the less one has, the more he becomes, and the greater his chance to be free.

Riding out Bellevue, I watched through my window for the towering gates of Rosecliff. As we approached, I asked the cabbie to slow, and he stopped at the foot of the drive. Through the gates, past the gardens, at the head of the drive, and beneath the rising sun, sat Rosecliff, draped like Elizabethan lace in the dew-kissed dawn.

Did anyone care, I wondered through the tears as the cab pulled away from the gate, or was love what befell the unfortunate ones, to become an unfortunate fate? What happened to Troy, to Mantua, to this glimmering town of dreams—to those who were offered love's sacrifice, and refused the chance to be great? What happened to this country, this century, this land, which began with such promise, such hope; what happened to these houses, to their men of industry, and their dreams that were all but gone?

We would never again see houses like this—not because we lacked the wealth, but because we lacked the dreams they took to raise them out of the rubble. If it was true that our future was gone with our past, Rosecliff had no place. Only Pickett made sense of it, and brought it back to life, to grace for an instant a century's end before we denied it again.

So, this was what drew him to the church, I thought, as I was leaving Newport behind. It was his sense of eternity, bound up in a past he believed could only return. If for him it was Athena he wanted most of all, for us it was the order restored—and the hope for a future awaiting us ahead, where we would find purpose once more.

For now we lived in a prideful time, when dreams were inherently beneath us. It was not only Pickett, but God Himself that we held in utter contempt, believing our works would trump any faith our naïve forbears could muster. Yet we had become the futureless fools, imprisoned by an empty present—of handshakes, arrogance, and finishing schools, which taught us not a thing.

The legacy we were leaving behind was the mediocrity of the middle. Gone were the palatial houses of Newport which had borne the dreams of this land, and come was the age of the condominium, of brick and wallboard and window plants, where we brokered our lives away. As babies of the post-war boom, we were the firstborn children of the bomb—inoculated by elixirs of success that insured we would never die—still, I couldn't help believing that beneath these lives, it was Pickett's for which we longed, and that one day we'd awake from intoxicated sleep to pursue our dreams again.

I realized then that Pickett was no less than destined to come from Six Bridges, for only from so humble a world-lost place could he have churned so great a dream. Only in the margins of a working-class life could he have known what it meant to work, reminding those of us who had never toiled a day of the sweat that had gotten us there. Whether it was Rosecliff or West of Broadway, it didn't seem to matter to him; there was no beginning or end to the dream—it was all the same to him.

Thinking back to his ingenious 'Trifecta', I longed for Pickett's innocence—of newspapers sold, to newspapers redeemed, to newspapers sold as fish wrap. The Adams had a different triangle trade: from molasses and rum; to trinkets and guns; to ammunition and slaves. As proud as I had been of the family legacy, for whatever good it had done, as the end of the line and a millennium, I was destined for the long way home.

Years later, I reached out a final time to my fading circle of friends, if only to indulge in disingenuous regret that they would never return. For I knew they would not, despite waxing poetic about my view of Étoile each night, washing my slanting apartment floor with its magnificent triumphal light. I knew the light had gone out of them, just as it had gone out of me—until the day I met John Pickett, and all he had hoped would be.

So came the time when I had to face the skeletons of my past, igniting a 'shot heard round the world' from a scandalized Adams clan. Surrendering my wealth didn't qualify as 'the honorable thing to do', because when all was said and done, the money was never rightfully mine in the first place. I already knew that our time had passed—if it had ever been—when we would be free of our legacy of demons to pursue the better angels of our nature.

With the help of an exploding worldwide web and a late-night Bourbon in hand, from time to time I undertook a search for traces of the erstwhile priest. For all the clever keywords, hyperlinks, tunneling, hunches, and cross-references, Pickett was as missing as an undercover agent in an eastern European country. The breakthrough came one Saturday night following an evening on the town—with raucous fellow journalists, nostalgically recounting uproarious stories of home—when, having regaled them with tales of Pickett and his unique journalistic effort, I went home to my laptop and typed into the engine the name of the paper, 'Spare Change'.

And lo and behold, it was very much alive. There, at the top of a sophisticated website, in elegant black and white, was a face I hadn't seen since that rain-soaked afternoon on the eve before leaving Newport. Beneath a photograph and his memorable smile, was inscribed, 'William Housch, Publisher'.

The site boasted a weekly circulation of eleven thousand papers, 'Sold by Vendors from West of Broadway to Anywhere West of Boston'. The online version featured local, national, and international news, arts and culture, and a front-page feature on issues of 'Social Justice'. Not that I expected Pickett to take credit for anything he had done, but there was nothing, even in 'Our History', that mentioned how the paper got started.

On the pretext of making my final bequest before closing my bank accounts, I flew to Boston, where curiosity got the better of me. Arriving in Newport, I looked in on my house, just to breathe in the ethers of the place—if not to bolster my courage to face what I feared was a tragic end. I went to the club for an early dinner and first had a drink at the bar, where from the lips of a gasping Winthrop Delafield, came the climax of the story.

Pickett lived in the Bishop's House in Providence. Athena had agreed to stay with Ted if he gave Pickett his ten-million-dollar take—and after a ferocious negotiation, Ted capitulated. Ted took a job as a tennis correspondent and they moved to California, where Elizabeth, with the gun unrecovered from Providence, shot herself.

The word was, Delafield zealously explained, Pickett was some kind of recluse. Yet his appearances occurred with such regularity that he was good for setting a watch. In the morning, one would have had to come to Newport, for at dawn he could be seen flying down Bellevue in the direction of West of Broadway, while in the evening it was at the Bishop's House, standing at the old stone gate.

It didn't take much to coax the details, fictional or not. Enacting the flight of an Aston Martin with the alacrity of a magician, Delafield's account transported me from Rosecliff to the gates of the Bishop's House. In the evening, the manse always brimmed with light—and absent as he was, one would nonetheless have guessed he had a party there every night.

As dusk was falling, I found myself rushing through an unwanted dinner, and before the waiter could offer dessert, I was already up from the table. I paid the check and passed through the lobby into the crisp fall night, hoping that as late as I knew it would be, I might get the chance to see Pickett. The traffic was heavy to Providence, despite my vehicular prayers; and by the time I arrived on the East Side, most of the evening was gone.

The gas lights burned on the cobbled street just as I remembered them, and I paused beneath my old front door before I turned the corner. I decided to park half a block shy of the illuminated Bishop's House, faithfully limned in the September cold and a gossamer veil of tears. Blinking to dispel my astonishment—and what could have been an apparition—Pickett was standing in the autumn night, there at the old stone gate.

He was looking up the empty street, as though he were awaiting someone, and then he looked down past my darkened car with that inimitably hopeful face. His inviolable faith, his unshakable belief that Athena was sure to come, was as clear to me as the truth that she would not, in love as she was with him. Dressed in his elegant double-breasted suit, his hair combed and shining in the light, Pickett hadn't changed an iota in the intervening years that I was gone.

I thought of the neighborhood Pickett came from, and those shattered mill town dreams, and the lovely house where he now lived, and the woman he had loved. It was all a part of the unending myth which lingers in every land— of paupers and kings, of human hope, and God-given destiny—yet it was Pickett who, by his audacity to dare the dream with his hands, had touched a life of love and longing which was uniquely American. Pickett brought it back by one shining ploy before the powers came down, to extinguish the light that threatened the darkness we all bore within.

Jealousy, pride, Ted's ignorant assumption that he was born to win, signaled the end of the life of a land whose humility had made it great. Pickett never believed he was born to win, and this was his victory. For unworthy and tired and a paperboy prince, he reached too far and was free.

I wanted to tell him I hated this time, and I almost got out of the car. But I knew he would only be mystified by why I was telling him this—by why our time even mattered to me in the face of what might be. For the first time I realized that he had always known the failings of our age, and that I had been the naive one where Ted and his world were concerned.

It was a fatal age of short-term commitments, and short-term memories, which could never have borne the eternal dreams that Pickett bore within. Only Pickett believed in a dream that transcended a century of wars, when we failed to see that in killing each other, we were finally killing ourselves. Only Pickett believed that the way to go on was the way of going back, and as I left him there at the gate, I knew he would be with me forever. It was a dream that reached back into a world of benevolent bishops and kings, where all that ever mattered was destiny, and the love that a young girl sings.